Reviews For *My Friend My Hero*

"I was glued...fascinated.

Fictional, yes, but it certainly keeps one focused on what is experienced in homes, schools and communities daily...A PICTURE OF LIFE.

The more things change, the more they look the same is applicable to the contents of My Friend My Hero. Mr. Hoover takes a harsh and penetrating look and gives a revealing portrait of the trials and tribulations of some of our youngsters. What is more, the book as written is easy to read but compelling and real, to which many can relate.

It is a story played out on the stage of life daily with the actors and actresses being our children, the future of America; the use and abuse of drugs and alcohol, the wasted talents, lives influenced and destroyed by external forces of evil, the pain and heartache of family and friends who suffer the immeasurable loss of what might have been.

This book should become classroom material, particularly for the thought-provoking questions posed at the end, an unusual feature in any book."

RONALD A. BLACKWOOD
Mayor of the city of Mount Vernon

"The message is clear as it delivers its lessons on living and inspires young people to truly live according to their beliefs, stand firmly on their own ground and not merely be a follower in the crowd."

MENTOR MAGAZINE

"A very courageous account of what it means to be a young person today. Hoover focuses on the importance of relationships, of staying in school, of fair play and setting positive goals. This is truly a story of self-respect and friendship woven with intelligence and maturity."

WILLIAM C. PRATELLA, Ph.D.
Superintendent of Schools—Mt. Vernon, NY

"My *Friend My Hero* is worth anyone's investment in the reading arena. It speaks not only to young hearts, but to all hearts, all ages and stages."

REV. DR. CECIL L. "CHIP" MURRAY
F.A.M.E. Church, Los Angeles, CA

"There's a little comedy, a little drama, a little suspense and a little mystery with the end result being...a story that is not only entertaining, but enlightening....My *Friend My Hero* is a wonderful first novel."

BLACKBOARD AFRICAN-
AMERICAN BESTSELLERS, INC.

"Congratulations on your remarkable book. It reaches into the soul and [it is] something that every young person should read. This book shows your remarkable ability as a writer. In my opinion, you deserve the Pulitzer Prize."

LADY D. MADISON
United House of Prayer

"A candid story of life and death. My *Friend My Hero* could be a fine tool for analytical problem solving dialog in any contemporary classroom."

MARCIA deCHADENEDES
Centrum Education Programs

"Kudos goes to Jerald LeVon Hoover for giving voice to the concerns which face our youth."

CHICAGO DEFENDER NEWSPAPER

"*My Friend My Hero* was like an overdue trip down memory lane with a powerful message!...REAL!...It's first class fiction with a message its readers cannot ignore!"

BILL DAUGHTRY
WFAN Radio

"This complex tale details the often difficult struggle faced by urban and rural teens seeking to avoid the perils of drugs and crime in the face of peer pressure and the desire to experience those forbidden fruits."

NORFOLK NEW JOURNAL AND GUIDE

"The style in which Mr. Hoover writes takes you back to the beginning and allows you to be brought into the future with a clear understanding of the world that these young unsung heroes are from...We see success measured in a new way."

J.E. ALSON-JOHNSON
James Weldon Johnson Community Centers, Inc.

"The lack of profanity and illicit connotations throughout the entire novel and the strong *anti-drug* and *Stay in School* message is in itself a very unique and refreshing experience."

SAINT LOUIS SENTINEL

"...an intriguing tale of realistic life in the projects. Hoover has the ability to transcend his readers into the minds, hearts and souls of these young African-American males. Their struggle and pursuit of happiness and their agony of defeat will keep you wrapped in the book until the very end..."

NEW PITTSBURGH COURIER

"Almost like tracing the path of hate changing into love, from young resentment to older understanding and forgiveness, My Friend My Hero is a map of travelling through the difficult years of growing up to a realization of the pressure faced by too many African-American families."

THE NEW YORK AMSTERDAM NEWS

MY FRIEND

MY HERO

Jerald LeVon Hoover

James C. Winston

Publishing Company, Inc.

Trade Division of Winston-Derek Publishers Group, Inc.

TO SOW THE FALLOW SOIL

First printing

PUBLISHED BY JAMES C. WINSTON PUBLISHING COMPANY, INC.
Trade Division of Winston-Derek Publishers Group, Inc.
Nashville, Tennessee 37205

Library of Congress Catalog Card No: 96-62093
ISBN: 1-55523-776-2

Printed in the United States of America

For my best friend in the
entire world...my son, Jordan.

And for my father for what
he went through in life inspired me to write.

PREFACE

My father Charles Levon Hoover passed away on April 20, 1989 at the age of 43. "Pop," as I affectionately called him, was some kinda guy. With his magnetic personality he could draw attention from anyone. Blessed with a multitude of gifts, he could carry on a conversation about anything. You name it and he knew something about it.

Pop was a great guy, but Pop was a drug and alcohol abuser. Those gifts he was blessed with were tarnished. No matter how much he knew, he could not put them to good use.

Yes, the question could be asked, "Why do people do drugs?" But, more importantly, the questions should be raised, "How can we help?" and "How can we put a stop to drugs?"

I know it's a delicate subject, one that cannot be easily talked about, especially with parents. I'll admit it was pretty hard for me, but I did it.

One cold January night, 1988, my wife and I were living with my father (my parents were divorced when I was six years old) and his folks in a three room apartment in the Bronx when Pop asked me, "What's wrong, baby?" "Baby" was the pet name used for everyone he loved.

"Nothin', Pop."

But he, knowing me for all of my twenty-two years, didn't believe me. "You sure?" he said.

"No…as a matter of fact, somethin' is wrong."

"What is it?" He took a seat across from me at the kitchen table.

"Pop," I said with all due respect, "you're on drugs and I don't like it."

His look was one of surprise and shock. "What'd you say, Jerald?"

"You're on drugs."

"Jerald, you don't know what you're talkin'…"

"I do, Pop." I had to interrupt him. "Because I know who got you into it and when you started on it."

He felt cornered. But he ever so humbly admitted, "You're right, Son." Water began to fill his eyes.

"You need help."

"Yeah, baby, I really have been tryin' to stop this junk but…"

"I know how it is." I didn't know from experience how it was, but I figured he was having a rough time.

We talked awhile, cried and hugged. He told me that he would go along with the help if I would make arrangements. I did make the arrangements, but he didn't hold to his end of the bargain.

By this time (February 1988), my wife and I had moved to upstate New York, and I refused to call him as often. Needless to say, I was very hurt and disappointed. I was never really ashamed of him, but not exactly proud either. My father's physical condition worsened, and he was in and out of the hospital for one reason or another.

But one day while lying in his hospital bed, something came over him. He said to a close friend of his, "You know, God has really been good to me." My father realized all this while taking medication for yet another illness.

"I feel like I'm at peace with God," my dad said, his voice filled with emotion. "Man, I don't want to be like this."

"You can make a change, Charles," his friend said.

"Yeah, I know. And before I take that stuff again, I'd rather God take my life. As soon as I get out of this hospital, I am gonna get back in church."

My dad made a change! He reacquainted himself with what he loved dearly in church: playing his musical instrument. But due to the nature of his illness, he was unable to perform the way he would've liked. But that didn't stop him. He became a spiritual booster. Charles LeVon Hoover bought himself a brand new reference Bible, a set of new shirts and ties, several pairs of shoes and a host of suits. He was always sharp as a tack.

Working in church and helping in areas that he really excelled in gave him great joy and satisfaction, so much so that he sought to expand his role there. What my dad aspired to do was to visit rehabilitation centers to teach the youth about the dangers of drugs, using himself as a living example. He also wanted to go to the street corners to catch those who had not yet begun to experiment with drugs to encourage them *not to do it*!

I'm proud of what my father wanted to do. He realized the life he lived was destroyed because of drug use and he wanted everyone else to realize that drugs are not the way to a healthy and productive life.

Pop, you may not have been Martin Luther King, Jr. or George Washington Carver, but in my book you're all right with me.

Young People—We Can Make A Difference
Don't Do Drugs!
Stay In School
Live And Be Somebody!

CHAPTER ONE

It's a warm mid-August day. The sun is shedding its light with three o'clock brightness over Fourth Street playground. Kirby sits, clad in his three-piece suit, white shirt and yellow tie, watching his two sons, eight-year-old Junior and seven-year-old Bennie, nearly have a Cain and Abel situation while playing hoops. "Knock it off, you two...play fair!"

"Yes, Daddy," Junior answers. "We're sorry."

Sensing an ease in tension, Kirby sits back to relax, only to be interrupted by his old high school buddy, Dexter.

"How've you been, Kirb? Haven't seen you in weeks."

"Oh, I've been taken it easy."

"Took the afternoon off?"

"Yeah, it's the weekend, wanted to get an early start. Besides," Kirby says with a laugh, "Kathy needed a break."

"Aw, she loves it," Dex says and gives Kirby a double-take. "Say man, when you gonna shave that stuff off your face?"

"Shave! It took me twenty-eight years to grow this. You remember how I was back then. I wasn't but a buck fifty, soaked and wet; had that bowl haircut, and wore those ugly, goofy lookin' glasses. I've got to enhance that image, man. Every time I see those old pictures, I cringe."

"I hear that."

"So, Mr. Brick Mason, how soon before that building on Columbus Avenue is finished?"

"I don't know," Dex says with a trace of frustration in his voice. "Every time we get to a point of finalizing, we get heavy rains."

Dex takes time to look at his surroundings and shakes his head in disgust. "Man, these projects sure ain't the same, since we lived in them."

"I know...You know something else?" Kirby says, his voice sounding a bit sorrowful. "Monday will be ten years."

Dex takes a deep breath and lets it out slowly. "Yeah, I know, '73. Seems like only yesterday."

"I can't believe Bennett's gone."

"I can't, either," Dex resumes the sigh.

"I remember that awful day like a book. I'll never get that waiting room out of my mind," Kirby murmurs, trying to hold back the tears. "Two drunks arguing over who had the most money and neither looked to have more than a dime in his pocket. That clock on that paint-chipped wall was twenty minutes slow, and the cushioned chairs had holes the size of my fist."

"Kirb, you really remember all that, too?"

"I bet if we were to go back there, we'd see those same two drunks, that same clock ticking too slow, and those same raggedy chairs."

"Don't forget the ugly receptionist," Dex says.

"With the deep voice!" the two men yell.

"It was just like the twilight zone," Kirby continues. "I can still remember that feeling of forgetfulness, a feeling of where-am-I, what-am-I-doing-here, sitting between the two girls, Kathy and Tara."

"Daddy! Look at this shot!" Bennie shouts.

"Very good, Son," Kirby calls, clapping his hands. He settles back onto the bench and thinks.

Bennett, I wish you were still here. Boy, do I miss you. The times we had in this park. I wish you could see my boys, how they're growing.

Every day they do something that reminds me of us. Wow! What friendship we had! We fought together, we fought with one another and we learned so much from one another. More important, we were always there for one another. What a time we had at those basketball games.

November 1972

They both played for Mt. Vernon High. Bennett was the star player. Kirby warmed the bench. Matter-of-fact, if it hadn't been for Bennett talking to Coach Dee, Kirby wouldn't have made the squad. At six-foot six, Bennett stood eight inches over Kirby.

He was a handsome, brown-eyed, lean and wiry type. He had long dangling arms that seemed to never end, his legs were like those of a thoroughbred race horse, and his massive hands allowed him to grip a basketball with just his thumb and pinky. He'd get this weird look on his face whenever he touched a basketball. It was so fierce it could've scared off a man-eating tiger. Coach Dee called it his "game face."

Their first game together was at home against arch rival New Rochelle High School. Bennett was his usual awesome self. The Mt. Vernon High sell-out crowd was thrilled by his slamdunking, magical passing, twenty-foot jump shooting with either hand and, of course, his strong defense that resulted in tons of blocked shots. There were quite a few college and professional scouts in the stands.

The seesaw game ended with Mt. Vernon winning 85-84. Bennett would always play the entire game and drop forty points easily. Kirby usually got playing time, in the final minutes, whenever there was a huge lead. He'd always manage to get into the scoring column, by notching two points. But, if he had a really good game, he'd score eight points. Kirby didn't mind the bench because he'd have a real ball acting puckish with the other players.

To Kirby, it was a pleasure just watching Bennett perform. Especially when the crowd got heated up, chanting, "BEN-nett, BEN-nett, BEN-nett!"

Whenever that happened, the opposition always seemed to self destruct. After a while, the chants turned into loud cheers, hoots and hollers because Bennett would come up with something spectacular. His favorite shot was a "tomahawk dunk."

Mt. Vernon High was, and still is, an average high school set in the center of an upper middle class neighborhood, in the boondocks surrounded by trees and historic houses. But the games were always something special. Special because of the tradition of its athletic accomplishments, and special because Bennett played there.

The moment you purchased your ticket, something exciting would happen. Just walking on the shiny wood gym floor, heat would burn your feet. The bleachers were always crawling with jubilant fans. And the intensity in the air was so thick, you could almost touch it.

There were even a few away games where the opposing crowds cheered for Bennett. That wasn't hard to understand. It was his personality that appealed to them most. Or maybe the folks of Mt. Vernon adored him so much that it became contagious. The four-and-a-half square mile town, just ten miles north of New York City and a stone's throw away from the Bronx, was a happening city.

That season was exciting. Before they knew it, the team was rolling with an 8-0 record. It was their best start ever, despite grumblings from several dissatisfied teammates. Bennett, along with his forty points per game average, was also tugging down twenty-three rebounds and handing out thirteen assists. *Bennett The Magnificent* was the nickname given him by the local press.

Bennett loved basketball, but he was also prominent in academics. That was very encouraging to the rest of the team. Easily an "A" student, he still, in Kirby's mind, was trying to keep up with Tara Copeland, the girl he had a thing for.

"Man, that girl is so fine. Long, black, silky smooth hair, dreamy brown eyes, soft caramel complexion and smart. How does she do it?" Bennett would say.

Though others might not've thought Tara was particularly interested in Bennett, Kirby knew, deep down, she fell for Bennett the moment she laid eyes on him. What girl didn't? Just to protect herself, she was determined not to fall prey to Bennett's charismatic charm.

He'd sit behind her in the chemistry classroom which resembled a laboratory with the long wooden table separating the class from Mr. Whitby, and stare at her through the entire lecture. She must've felt heat on the back of her neck, from Bennett's penetrating gaze.

At lunch, he'd sit with the gang—the gang being Bennett, Kirby, Big Joe and Dex—and not touch his food. He'd stare at Tara, sitting with her friends from the Honor Society.

"Bennett, are you fastin' or are you on a food strike or what?" Paying little attention to what Kirby asked, he'd answer, "Yeah, Kirby, yeah. That's right, yeah, yeah." Kirby thought he was going crazy for a while because so many other girls liked the man. They practically threw themselves at him, he wanted Tara who played hard to get. Kirby couldn't quite figure that out.

They'd go to Kirby's house—a two-bedroom apartment—in the projects. Bennett talked about Tara from the time he stepped in till the time he stepped out.

"Tara is so fine. Man, that girl is fine. You watch Kirby, you watch. In time she'll be mine."

"She wouldn't go with you to a soup line, if she was starvin'." Bennett, slightly angered, punched Kirby in the leg, giving him such a charley horse that Kirby's whole right side went numb.

Kirby really had confidence that Bennett could eventually crack Tara's shell. When and how, was another question.

In their senior year, before they fell in love, inviting Tara to games seemed useless to Bennett. She'd say stuff like, "I don't want to see a bunch of oversized adolescents running around in shorts chasing after a ball." But, no matter how much Bennett was insulted, he never conceded.

Some days he'd beat Tara to Mr. Whitby's chemistry class, just so he could write anonymous notes on the blackboard. It was evident Bennett was the guilty one, he being the only student wearing chalk dust.

Those weren't the only messages she received from him. While at the lunch table starving himself half to death, he'd write and then pass her little heart-shaped notes.

Like most females who had just received a love letter she'd blush, then she'd tuck it into one of her books, without giving poor Bennett any other sign of encouragement.

He went through an awful lot to capture her heart. But, there was one day when, if she wasn't careful playing that hard-to-get routine, she would've lost him for sure. It was on a Friday, there was no game or practice because of a coaches' meeting. Bennett decided, on his own, he'd walk her home.

While they walked, Bennett pleaded, "Please, go out with me Tara, just once."

"No, Bennett, I won't."

"Come on, baby...Why not?" Bennett asked innocently.

"Because."

"Because what?"

"Because, I said so!"

"Is it because I'm tall, dark, and handsome?"

She looked at him like he was from another planet. "No!"

"Well, what is it then, Tara. Is it because I live in the projects and you live…"

"No, Bennett, it's nothing like that."

Tara started to laugh, but before she could get a word in edgewise, she noticed Bennett was looking around for the source of the unwelcomed scent in the air. Tara began to sniff and then they saw it: dog mess on the tip of Bennett's left sneaker. He made an about-face and saw there was a trail from where he had stepped in it, several yards back. His heart stopped. His head felt like it weighed a ton, and to see Tara laughing uncontrollably, only made matters worse. The most embarrassing moment in his life. He dashed away, yelling, "I'll never speak to you again, Tara, never again!" Tara kept walking, still hysterical.

That night Bennett went downstairs to Kirby's fourth floor apartment, a crushed man. When Kirby first saw him, he wondered if he'd been in a fight. He knew Bennett had a quick temper, but he'd fight only if thoroughly pushed. Besides, he wouldn't have fought without Kirby at his side. So he abandoned the thought.

"What in the world happened to you?"

Bennett walked in and sat at the kitchen table. "I stepped in some dog-crap, while I was walkin' Tara home, and she laughed at me, man."

Kirby had to fight for all he was worth—and then some—just to keep from cracking a smile. He was afraid, if he was to even look amused, Bennett would mop up the floor with him.

It finally hit Kirby that after all of Bennett's hunger strikes, novel writings, and mood swings, Bennett was in love. He decided he'd get Bennett and Tara together once and for all. He wanted to do it right away.

"Man, you look, a mess. Why don't you go home and get some sleep. Things will be okay in the mornin'."

"Yeah, Kirby, I am tired. But, things won't be better, in the mornin'. I can tell you that. Later."

The door slammed. Kirby jumped out of his pj's and into his street gear. As Kirby proceeded to get dressed, he couldn't help but feel satisfaction in knowing that he was doing all that he could do to secure his buddy's happiness. Just two years ago, it was Bennett who saved Kirby from nearly ruining his life—dealing in drugs.

Money was scarce in the Maxwell household, due to the fact that Kirby's father was unemployed, and there were five mouths to feed. Kirby felt it was his duty to become a breadwinner, so he opted for the quick fix.

Angela lived in the next building. Angela and Tara were in the Honor Society together. Angela was treasurer. She was one of those girls that threw herself at Bennett too. But Kirby didn't care. He needed her.

She, like Bennett, lived on the tenth floor, and since the elevators in her building were generally out of order, he instinctively ran up the stairs. As usual, the stairway stunk of urine, and there was so much graffiti on the walls, you couldn't tell their original color.

When he reached his destination, he grabbed both calves as he bent over to catch his breath.

"Who is it?" Angela said.

"It's Kirby!"

"Kirby? Why on earth are you knocking on my door, this time of night?"

"It's an emergency! Can I please come in?"

"This better be good."

Angela's apartment reminded Kirby of his own with all the pictures, plates and other painted pottery on the walls. Her place had three bedrooms, and there was no carpeting. That reminded him of Bennett's place. A good thing, because the nightgown Angela was wearing sure looked good, and almost made him forget why he was there—Angela was a fox. Every time Kirby saw her he thought of how lucky Bennett might've been or how stupid he is now.

"You home alone?" He smiled and sat on the plastic covered blue velvet couch.

"No," she said. "My father is asleep in the back, and he has a gun under his pillow."

"Very funny," Kirby responded.

"Well, what's the big emergency?"

"Angela...can I have Tara's phone number?"

She wavered, then shook her head. "I knew it! Kirby can't you see Tara doesn't want Bennett."

"Never mind, it's no use...sorry I asked." Kirby started for the door. He turned when Angela yelled, "Wait! I'll give it to you. I guess I don't have anything to gain by not giving it to you. It's in my phone book in the back."

He smiled to himself. *You're on your way, Bennett. You're on your way.*

Moments later, Kirby was home dialing the number. The phone rang several times before a woman answered.

"Hello."

"Hello, Mrs. Copeland?...Tara?"

"Yes, this is Tara."

"This is Kirby."

"Kirby who? Bennett's friend?"

"Yeah."

"Do you know what time it is? And how'd you get my number?"

"Yeah, I know what time it is," Kirby answered, ignoring the latter question. "But this is important. It's about Bennett."

"I kinda figured that."

"You know he's in love with you, right?"

"Love?"

"Yes. It's been a year and a half since you moved here from Chicago, and he's chased you since day one. Why are you treatin' him so badly?"

"For starters, Kirby, I feel for him the same way he feels for me."

"You do?"

"Yes, but I refuse to make a fool of myself. It's bad enough, having all these girls disliking me, for no apparent reason."

"Tara, did you plan on tellin' him this?"

"Yes, eventually. As a matter-of-fact today. But, before I could, Bennett stepped in..."

"Tara," Kirby said with a smile, "you don't have to tell me. I know what happened."

"You do, do you?" In an attempt to muffle her laugh, Tara placed her hand over her mouth.

"I know you couldn't help laughin'. I cracked up inside and I'm his best friend. But, you'd better think of somethin' good and fast, because he's had just about enough of your stubbornness."

"I'm sure. But, don't worry. I'll take care of things on Monday."

"Monday? Why not tomorrow? Or tonight? That would be even better."

"Because, I have to go to Connecticut tomorrow, and won't be back until late Sunday night at the earliest. And tonight is out of the question. Besides, I'm worth the wait."

"Okay," Kirby said with a laugh. "Monday it is. I'm not tellin' Bennett I spoke to you about this."

"You better not."

"Yeah, right," Kirby said, fully relieved about the agony his buddy was feeling. "Okay, Tara, see you Monday."

Tara came to school that Monday wearing a sexy black and white dress with a pearl necklace and earrings, suede black shoes, and a matching purse. Her perfume was so strong that it left a scented trail from the moment she entered the building. She walked into chemistry class and was greeted by Mr. Whitby who was sporting his usual high-water pants, short-sleeved shirt, bow tie and Coke-bottle-thick glasses. "Hello, Mr. Whitby."

He responded in his resonant voice, "Hello sweetie. My, you look nice this morning!"

"Thank you." Tara looked to the blackboard, but wasn't surprised to see nothing from Bennett. She elegantly took her seat in front of him, while he pretended to read. Wouldn't you know it! The book was upside down!

Normally, whenever Tara first sat down, she'd start copying Mr. Whitby's notes. But, this day was different.

She began writing on notepad paper.

Dear Bennett,

How was your weekend? Was it like mine, miserable? I hope not. Because if it was, I know I'm the cause of it. Please forgive me. I realize now I was very wrong in hurting you. I'm also glad for me in catching myself in time because, if I hadn't, I would've been very sorry for the rest of my life. The truth is that I started liking you when I first moved here, a year and a half ago. I couldn't show it. Not that I was being stubborn, but because I didn't want to be just another girl to you if we ever met. Please understand. And I'd love to go out on a date with you, anytime you set. You'll have to meet my parents first. I'm sure they'll like you.

Love, Tara
P.S. Does your foot still stink? Ha! Ha!

Tara slipped the letter underneath the desk to Bennett who gawked at her with his mouth open. "All right!"

"Son," a startled Mr. Whitby said, "what's gotten into you? You know better than that." By this time all the class' attention had reverted to Bennett who was grinning from ear to ear. "I don't tolerate that in my class," Mr. Whitby continued. "Now, take your books, and your belongings, and excuse yourself. I will not have that, and is that clear to the rest of you?"

"Yessir, Mr. Whitby," the entire class answered. The students got an extra kick out of Bennett, when he stumbled to the floor trying to get up from his desk. He left the classroom shouting to Tara, "You'll never regret it! I promise, you'll never regret it! Wow! I'm in love!" Bennett left Tara giddy as a kid eating candy.

That same day during basketball practice, Bennett was playing like a man possessed. He always gave one hundred percent, but love gave him extra power that day.

"Congratulations, man." Kirby patted Bennett on his sweaty thigh, while they sat in the locker room after their workout.

"What's wrong?" Kirby asked. "Don't tell me. You're pregnant."

"No man, stop kiddin' around. I did somethin' real dumb."

"What?"

"I finally have a date with the most beautiful girl on the planet, and I ain't got the first means of employment."

The following two weeks, Bennett walked Tara home. Of course, this time, they walked on the other side of the street. They made googlie-eyes at one another, so much so, people thought they were nuts.

Walking her home also meant dinner at her house. With his appetite back, he loved it. But, he didn't particularly love being nicknamed *Ben Copeland* by his teammates.

CHAPTER TWO

On Friday, January 4, 1973, Mt. Vernon had a home game against DeWitt Clinton High School. Before the game, the Knights assembled in the team meeting room. The room had a huge brown wooden table that made it difficult to move around and a chalkboard that Coach Dee used to diagram plays. The lights were always dim, and the smell reminded you of the zoo.

Some of the guys waltzed into the room clowning in a feminine-like manner:

"Hey baby!" one voice cried out.

"Honeybuns, come here," someone demanded.

"No sugar, you come here," another voice begged.

Bennett and Big Joe looked at them like they were crazy.

The team settled down and Bennett, the captain, started the meeting. Bennett wasn't the team captain just because of his awesome abilities on the basketball court, he was also a natural leader. Having been thrust into the dual roles of first-born son and man of the house made him an insightful young man.

"Fellas, it appears as though we'll be goin' to Glen Falls for the state championship. But that means we have to win at least four of our last six games. I know we can do it. I don't know if you've read the papers, but we're favored to win it all. Our record is 17-2—we lost two in a row. I know our shootin' was off against St. Anthony's and I was in foul trouble the last game, we should've pulled them off, anyway. I'm not blamin' anybody, so no one should feel singled out."

Coach Dee walked in. Coach's real name was William O'Brien, but they called him Coach Dee because he was so strict about playing defense.

"Excuse me, Coach, but I'd like to continue on if I may?" Coach nodded.

"It appears to be a little tension in the air. If there's someone, anyone on this team havin' somethin' against another player, please get it straightened out. And, let's knock off the backbitin' and bickerin'. A house divided can't stand and the same goes for a team. We can't make it without togetherness. We should all be about team; team first and team last."

The room was quiet, like a library, until a voice shouted, "I got somethin' to say." Hezekiah, the team preacher man, was on his feet. Hezekiah wore nothing but suits, shirts and ties to school and every so often on the team bus, during quiet times, he'd be found reading scriptures.

"Personally," Hezekiah continued, "I feel like I should be gettin' more playing time. I felt this way at the beginnin' of the season. Now we're headed toward the end of it. I'm a senior, one of only six. Four seniors start. I realize that I'm not the most gifted player, but I feel I should be gettin' more P.T. than a sophomore. I have nothin' personal against Honey Jack or even you, Coach, but he's only a sophomore and that's how I feel."

Coach Dee understood what Hezekiah was saying, and he agreed.

The coach had been a three-sport star back in the early 50s. He was a tall man; he stood six feet seven. He had blonde hair and blue eyes, and he walked with a slight limp. He still maintained his shooting touch, though. In fact, he sometimes outshot Bennett in practice. That is, whenever his arthritis didn't act up.

"Hez, since you were man enough to tell me your feelings, I will make sure you get more playing time. But this doesn't mean every guy who isn't satisfied with his P.T. will get more. Hezy is extremely dedicated to this team, and if some of you would follow his example, we'd be an even better team then we are now."

The coaching staff and the players as a whole felt as if a weight had been lifted off their shoulders.

"Wait, I have somethin' to say," Kirby said.

"What is it?" Coach's look said, Is this guy for real?

Kirby stood up, "Just give me a moment, I'll tell you."

"Come on Kirby, what is it?" one of the assistant coaches asked.

Kirby played like he was dancing and holding someone said, "I still get a rush every time I watch the "Julia Show" and see that fine Diahann Carroll walkin' around in that nurse's uniform."

"You, are one, sick puppy," someone said.

Everyone got a kick out of that and some of the fellas threw their towels and wristbands at him.

When the team settled down, Coach delivered his speech, pointing out weaknesses in DeWitt Clinton's team.

He ended like always, "Let's get 'em!"

When they ran down from the locker room onto the basketball court for their warm-up drill, the crowd rocked.

The starting five were: Bennett; the other forward at six-feet-five, Ronnie O'Koren; six-feet-eight center, Big Joe Hancock; Dexter Stratton, who at six-two looked a lot like Bennett, walked a lot like Bennett and even tried to talk like Bennett, and was also the best defensive player at shooting guard; and last, at six-one, the point guard, Davey "Honey Jack" Sanchez. Honey Jack took over the starting guard spot once manned by Leonard "Stinky" Robinson, who was kicked off the team for disciplinary reasons and subsequently dropped out of school. Then came the rest of the bunch: freshman Jeffrey Bryce Frazier (if the guys didn't know any better, they'd swear his parents were brother and sister); John Berry, the "Great White Hope," so nicknamed because he'd always bring the team pastry from his parents' bakery; Jeff Kendall, the quiet one on the team whose his ears were the size of bird wings; skinny

Brandon "Petty Cash" Jones, the money man; Stanley Rowinsky, the team's tallest guy with legs that formed the letter "K" whenever he stood still; and Hezekiah and Kirby.

They killed DeWitt Clinton, 107-45. Bennett scored his usual forty, and Kirby got lucky and hit nine.

The next Friday, January 11, 1973 was a home game against Riverdale High School and they won 95-93 on Bennett's last-second fifteen-foot jump shot. The buzzer sounded and the team charged and jumped all over him. Making their way back to the locker room, Bennett was approached by a slender-framed, mischievous-looking male. The man had been standing with "Stinky" near the exit. He wore a long, dark green leather coat with a white fur collar, a dark green velvet hat rimmed with powder white fur and a black patch over his right eye. The instant Kirby laid eyes on him, he thought he was a no account.

When Bennett walked into the locker room several minutes later, Kirby asked, "What did that guy want?"

Soaked with sweat, he started undressing. An incredulous look was on his face. "Stinky introduced us and he said to me, if I want to be rich, then lose the next game."

That's when Kirby knew why he had that uncomfortable feeling. The guy was a hustler, and wanted Bennett to be his patsy.

"Well, are you goin' to talk to him or what?" Bennett, somewhat insulted, gave Kirby a look.

"Now, Kirby, come on. Give me a break."

Kirby thought of the harm the man could do to Bennett's career, if he were to become corrupt. "Bennett, I don't like the sound of this. 'Be rich, lose next game.' This guy is bad news."

"Kirby, please."

"Well, just look at what's happened to Stinky. He was All-County and All-State one year, and a complete bum the next."

"Stinky just introduced us. Besides, I've never seen that guy before in my life. How could he have anythin' to do with Stinky not playing ball? Stinky has other problems, too, you know." Kirby released a sigh, as he shut his locker.

"I guess you're right about Stinky...but, I still don't like this guy."

"Look, Kirb, let's discuss this later."

CHAPTER THREE

"Hey, Tara, Sol. It's five o'clock. Is this meetin' over with yet?" Bennett walked into the classroom.

"Coming right now, hon," Tara said.

Tara was vice president of the Honor Society and Sol Weiss was president. This drove Bennett nuts, because the two would sometimes spend countless hours together studying or tossing around ideas after Honor Society meetings. Sol drove a serious sports car, wore nice clothes, had a pocketful of money, was smart and very personable. He had the kind of eyes that made girls get crazy. He was a handsome dude, according to them.

"See you tomorrow, Tara," Sol said and gathered his books.

"Yeah." Bennett watched Sol as he left the classroom. "I don't like you with Sol."

"Why not?"

"Because, he's sneaky. I don't like his eyes."

"You're being ridiculous, Bennett. I don't tell you I don't want you playing basketball because of those cheerleaders, do I?"

"So," Bennett shrugged.

"That's not fair. Bennett, you're jealous. And, for what, I don't know."

"Okay," Bennett said. "Besides," his look was sly when he folded his arms, grinned and said, "this guy asked me the other day if I wanted to be rich."

"Excuse me?"

"Nothin'. Nothin' at all. Let's go."

⟡

A few nights later, Bennett woke up around three o'clock in the morning to go to the bathroom. He saw his mother sitting on her bed, crying. She had just gotten home from her factory job and didn't hear him get up. While watching from the dark hallway, Bennett noticed her tremble.

"Momma," Bennett whispered as he entered her room, "you're crying. Somethin's wrong, tell me about it." He sat down and put his arms around her. "Momma, tell me what's wrong."

Mrs. Wilson waited a while before speaking in a muffled voice. "Son, I hurt, and my body is very tired. The doctor told me my blood pressure was much too high when I went to the clinic yesterday. The doctor also told me I need to get more rest. But, I can't rest too much now. I gotta go to work. I can't get disability and we can't get welfare because they say I make too much money. As it is, I'm already two months behind in the rent."

"Momma, I love you."

"I love you, too, Son."

"Momma, I'll quit school and get a job, a real good one."

"No, Bennett."

"But..."

"No, I said. You're not gonna quit no school to get no job. Do you hear me?"

"Yes, Momma," he said.

"You go on to bed. It's late. Everything will be taken care of. Don't worry."

"Yes, Momma, good night."

"Good night, baby, and close the door on your way out."

He stood outside the door, listening to his mother. His eyes filled; he had lost his urge to go to the bathroom. He went to check on the other two Wilsons in the house, Yvette and Dannon.

Yvette, his sister, was pretty with thick beautiful braids and remarkably mature for thirteen. And Dannon, his brother, eight years old, terribly short and light-complexioned, in total contrast to the rest of the family. Yvette and Dannon slept in the next room. Looking in on them, he couldn't help but break into tears. He went back to bed trying to think of a way to help his family.

He woke up from his three-hour nap with fire in his eyes. "I'm gonna, get me a job." He wasn't going to disobey his mother by quitting school. He decided to quit the team instead.

He walked up and down the streets of busy downtown Mt. Vernon. He searched the stores hoping someone might be hiring students for after-school work. He checked hardware stores, sporting goods stores, paint stores. But he couldn't find a thing until he decided to change to another avenue. That's when he spotted the HELP WANTED sign in the window of Hamburger Haven.

"It's crowded in here," Bennett said upon entering the greasy spoon.

The front had high bar-room stools at the counter, and the back was filled with brown table-and-chair combos. The large crowd certainly did nothing to change his mind about wanting to work. Hard work never intimidated him.

He snatched the sign from the window and walked over to a well groomed gentleman, who he figured to be in charge. The man was wearing a shirt and tie. Bennett approached him with a smile. "Excuse me, I'm here in response to your job posting."

"So you are," the man said and began pulling on his beard. "Don't I know you from somewhere?"

"I don't know..."

"Got it! You're Bennett Wilson, that basketball player!"

"Yes, sir, I am." Bennett's smile widened.

"So you want a job, huh?"

"Yes, sir, somethin' for after school or evenin'."

"First of all, drop the 'sir'; my name is William Harper, but call me Bill," he said. "I'm the manager."

Harper pulled out a notebook and flipped through the pages. "I need someone from eight to two Monday through Friday, and every other Saturday from nine to four. Think you can handle that?"

"Yes, sir...I mean Bill."

Two men, vestured in construction gear, walked in and noticed Bennett. "Ay, Bennett! Go get em, star."

"I see you have fans," Bill said.

"Who, me? Nah."

"Well, get this, celebrity," Bill said smiling and looking up at Bennett, "you be here at seven so you can be fitted for a uniform. I think we'll find one that fits."

"I hope so but, I start tonight? What exactly do I do?"

"You know how to make burgers?"

"Yes."

"You know how to sweep?"

"Yes."

"Well, my friend, there's your answer and you'll get $2.90 an hour."

"Thanks!" The two gentlemen shook hands again and Bennett charged away. He was at the door when he heard Bill say, "And don't fool around with the waitresses!"

On the way home, Bennett was beaming at everything: storefronts, people snuggled under their coats, car horns honking, cars parking, lights changing. When he reached the building, he ran into Mrs. Smith, the oldest tenant in the complex.

"Could I take one of those for you, ma'am?"

Mrs. Smith, who also acted as the building's baby sitter peered at him over her grocery bags. "No, thank you, Bennett. My, you are looking sanguine today."

"Sanguine, ma'am?"

"Happy, dear, happy. Well...who is she?"

"What? Oh no, ma'am. I just got a job. That's why I'm so...sanguine." The two shared a brief chuckle.

"Well, congratulations. Your mother will be proud."

"Yes, ma'am, I sure hope so. Oh, could you hold the elevator for me? I forgot to check my mail."

"Okay, but hurry. I have my children upstairs."

Bennett opened the mailbox. Envelopes poured out onto the floor. Mrs. Smith put her grocery bags down in front of the elevator door and helped him gather them up.

"Georgetown University," she said, glancing at one of the letters. "Norfolk State, UCLA, Howard, Yale, Morehouse, Morgan State University...good heavens...University of Alberta. Bennett, are these all for you?"

"Yes, ma'am."

"My, your mother must be proud!"

When Bennett arrived at his apartment, he had to kick on the door. His mother opened it. "My God, where did all the mail come from? And what are you doin' home so early?"

He ran to the kitchen table and dropped the mail like a sack of potatoes.

"Guess what, Momma? I got a job!"

"Now, Bennett, I told you last night you wasn't gonna quit no school to work!"

"Yes, Momma, but..."

"But...I told you last..."

"Momma, I didn't quit school!" Bennett shouted then instantly calmed himself. "This is an after-school job."

"After school? But, you play ball after school!"

"Yes, I know and I can still do that."

"How, if you work? Son, you know the only way you're gonna get into a decent college is with a scholarship."

"I work from eight at night till two in the mornin' and on Saturdays. See, I can work, still go to school and play ball."

"You gotta work Saturday, too?"

"Only every other Saturday."

"Son, how you gonna do all this durin' school?"

"I know it sounds hard, but I can do it. I just want to help you and make things better for myself. Momma, I have four pairs of pants and three of them are dungarees. I'm so tall now, you can't buy clothes for me anymore. Momma, please let me work! Please!"

"I don't know, Son."

"But, Momma, I have to start tonight."

"Tonight!"

"Yes, Momma, tonight. Please?"

"Okay, Son," Mrs. Wilson sighed. "You better go get some rest now."

"Thanks, Momma," He kissed her, then remembered "the letter." Bennett fished through the mass of envelopes on the table looking for "the letter." A letter from Columbia University in New York City.

"I got it, I got it! Momma, I got it! I got the scholarship! Yes! I got it!"

"Son, calm down and read the letter first."

"Momma," an exuberant Bennett said, "they're sayin' they would put me in a work-study program." Bennett continued to read the letter and as he concluded each sentence, his smiled widened. "Momma, I got it!"

He grabbed his mother and danced her around the kitchen. His two-step would've made Fred Astaire and Ginger Rogers proud. "Tara...I must go tell my sweetie."

Mrs. Wilson, a round and chunky woman with tiny moles on her face and neck and a head full of gray hair, stood against the refrigerator watching proudly. He went into the bathroom and seconds later rushed out like a bull chasing a matador.

"See you later, Momma."

He ran downstairs to Kirby's apartment.

"Kirb, Kirb!"

"Yeah, what's up?" Kirby seemed startled.

"I got a job. I also got that scholarship to Columbia!"

"All right Ben-Ben!" The two slapped five. "But Bennett, how you gonna work, go to school and play ball?"

"Don't worry, everything is straightened out," Bennett said, not wanting to go through that scene again.

"I hope so."

"Stop worryin'," he said as he looked in the mirror in the living room. "Did you see my girl today?"

"Yeah, I saw her briefly. She was with that guy Sol."

"And what's wrong with you? I'm the one that should be lookin' miserable, if anybody."

CHAPTER FOUR

"Hi, Mrs. Copeland." Bennett flashed a false smile. "Is Tara home?"

"No, dear, she isn't. But you can come in and wait for her."

"Okay, thank you. I'll do that."

Mrs. Copeland was naturally beautiful. She, like Tara, had that soft caramel complexion. She was on the chubby side like Bennett's mother, but she sported all the "in" fashion threads, and she had those luscious, fat, kissy cheeks that dimpled whenever she cracked a smile. She was generally home during the day. Her husband didn't want her working because he was very successful in his construction business and felt that his woman's place was...well...in a word...home. All in all, the Copelands were the type of parents you'd love to have. The kind that thought they were still young. Tara's father, nicknamed "Tim-Tim," was also the neighborhood comedian. He kept everybody in stitches.

"Would you like something to eat while you're waiting?"

"No, Mrs. Copeland, I'm fine, thanks."

Bennett sat on the couch with a *Jet* magazine in his hand. Whenever he was there, he always admired the big green and white house which in the affluent section of Mt. Vernon. Mrs. Copeland loved plants and they sprawled in every room of the abode, except Tara's. She didn't want the responsibility of taking care of them.

An hour and a half went by. Hence, having read eight *Jet* magazines, his patience exhausted completely, Bennett rose from the couch and started for the door. Mrs. Copeland followed him. He opened it and saw Tara getting out of Sol's car. As always, Sol peeled off at the sight of him.

Mrs. Copeland, feeling tension in the room, did an about-face and hurried upstairs. When Tara reached the door, he greeted her with a hostile, "It's about time."

"What are you talking about?" she said, placing her books on the table in the foyer.

"Come on, Bennett. You know I have meetings after school. Please, honey. Let's not fight."

"I'll always feel the way I feel. But that's not what I came here for. I have great news," he beamed. "I got a job."

"That's great!"

"And, I also got that scholarship to Columbia."

"Yeah, that's good," she said, but a bit deflated.

"What's wrong, Tara?"

"Nothing's wrong. It's just...Oh, I don't know."

"Come on, Tara." Bennett embraced her. "You just cheered me up."

"I'm okay," she said through a false smile.

"Hey, babe, let's go get somethin' to eat at Mickey Dee's."

The next day was Thursday, the day before an important game against New Rochelle High. Bennett, Big Joe, Dex and Kirby were sitting in the lunchroom. The lunchroom was half the size of a football field, endowed with water fountains, long battered tables and plastic seats in outrageous colors. On the walls were pictures of past principals, scholars and former athletes.

"This food sucks!" Kirby shouted at the top of his lungs. "Tough overcooked chicken, nasty mashed potatoes, greasy string beans, sour milk and look at this...rotten fruit!"

Bennett and the rest of the crew seemed to take it in stride, but not Kirby. He found it totally unforgivable for a school to serve such bad food.

He checked first to see if anyone was watching. Then he flung his chicken leg across the cafeteria. Angered at Kirby, Bennett snapped, "Hey man, are you crazy?" Kirby, didn't respond, but instead reached for his milk and flung it across another part of the cafeteria. Milk was splattered all over the place. As it would happen, students broke and started throwing food from all directions. Kirby said to himself, Oh no, what did I start?

With a headlock, Bennett tried to restrain Kirby from throwing anymore food. Kirby broke free from Bennett's grip and ran, grabbing yet another piece of chicken. Bennett looked right silly trying to catch Kirby while bobbing and weaving from the flying food. The chase finally ended when Kirby ran over a monitor like a fullback, knocking him to the floor.

Bennett grabbed Kirby's collar with one hand and snatched the chicken with the other. At that instant the monitor looked up and spotted Kirby and Bennett. Bennett was holding the evidence. The monitor, who doubled as a bouncer at a local bar, got to his feet and grabbed them both by their jackets.

"Okay, you two, you're goin' to Principal Lazarus' office."

"But I..." Bennett said.

"Never mind, superstar."

The monitor dragged Bennett and Kirby off to see the principal.

Principal Lazarus was a slender man about five-five, without his high-heeled boots.

He was freckled, looked like the cartoon character Porky Pig and had brown, sometimes red hair, depending on what color dye was on sale.

Bennett and Kirby sat side by side, the monitor towering over them. The office smelled of mint. The thick beige rug made them feel like they were walking on air the way it cuddled their feet. The bone colored-cushioned chairs resembled huge pillows and the big brown desk with the sheet of glass covered photos of old movie stars. Old Lazarus had the best layout in town. Bette Davis, Clark Gable, Jack Benny, you name them, they were there.

Lazarus sat behind his desk, absorbed in the story. "Wilson, I'm really shocked to discover that you were engaged in such a fracas."

Bennett responded, "Sir, I wasn't in it. I was just tryin' to stop it."

"You were trying to stop it, huh, with food in your hands? Please! What kind of fool do you take me for?"

"The food was in my hand because I snatched it from someone else. And as for my clothes, I got hit a few times."

Kirby was surprised Bennett didn't tell on him, but figured he knew what he was doing. He felt terrible, but thought how much of a good friend Bennett was.

"Due to the nature of the situation," Principal Lazarus spoke as a judge handing down his sentence, "I find it in the best interest that you two be suspended for one day. Effective immediately."

"In whose best interest?" Bennett said.

"Wilson!" Principal Lazarus shot back, "I think you've said enough."

"Suspended!" Bennett shouted. "We got a big game tomorrow!"

"I've made my decision. The case is closed."

Boy, was Bennett upset. Kirby didn't know whether he was madder at him or at Lazarus. For Bennett's sake only, Kirby tried taking full blame. It was no use. With blood in their eyes they stormed out of the office.

"I can't believe Lazarus," Bennett said.

"Yeah. I hope he dies with his boots on."

It was a long, cold walk home.

It got even chillier when they bumped into Stinky hanging on the corner of Ninth Street and Third Avenue—just down the block from where they lived. Ninth Street was more famous for being a drug haven than a regular residential and commercial enterprise. For a radius of nearly six blocks, you could duck into almost any apartment building and find a drug house with dealers ready, willing and able to supply your drug of choice.

"What's up, Stink?" Bennett greeted him as the two slapped five.

"Hey, Ben-Ben, what it is?...Oh, what's up, Kirby?"

"Nothin', dope fiend...Absolutely nothin'."

"Kirb, lighten' up," Bennett said.

"That's okay, I'm cool!"

"You're not cool! You're a junkie!"

"Relax, Kirby," Bennett said.

"No! Just look at him! His clothes are filthy, he's shakin' like a leaf, he smells, and look at his eyes...He's a complete mess!"

"Leave, Kirby! Go home!...Now!"

"Look at him, Bennett! Just look at him. He could've been one of the best ball players around, but no!"

"Kirb, I said, split. Go home. I'll handle this!"

"What, a waste of talent," Kirby said and walked off.

"Sorry, Stink, you know how he gets. He's just a little upset, that's..."

"I'm not. Don't worry about it." Bennett and Stinky exchanged fives. Stinky then reached into his jacket. "Here, Ben, some *get high*." *Get high* was a colloquialism for marijuana.

"What! No!...Give me that, fool!"

"Step back, Bennett." Stinky embraced the garbage just before putting it back into his pocket.

"Stinky."

"I'm flyin' high, man." Stinky flapped his arms in jest.

"What!"

"I feel like you when you go up for one of those fabulous dunk shots...*swoosh!*"

"Stinky, why are you doin' this? You're hurtin' yourself, and so many people. Your family..."

"My family!...Did you not forget? I'm an only child, and my daddy's dead. Dead, seven years."

"Your mother's hurt! The team's hurtin'! Man, we all love you. What is it?"

"Man, I don't care," Stinky said and waved Bennett off. "I'm real nice right now, real nice. In my own world!"

"Stinky," Bennett chased behind him, "you got no business bein' like this. No business. Man, get back in school, rejoin the team and get yourself together. You'll still have another year left. Possibilities for a scholarship still exist. Come on, Kirby's right, you could be one of the best..."

"Look, I don't need you preachin' to me."

"I'm not preachin' to you, man!" Bennett grabbed Stinky by the arm. "Hey, I'm not without my problems. I'm on suspension for a game."

"Oh, yeah!" Stinky responded in surprise. "What happened?"

"Long story. I'll tell you some other time."

"Suspension."

"Look, I'm comin' to you as my friend, my partner...my main man. You know that. Shoot! We live right across the hall from one another. We grew up together. We've always been close. We talked all the time."

"Did you ever try talkin' to your no 'count, in-and-out-of-prison, no payin' child support, alcoholic daddy? You wanna rehabilitate everybody!"

"That, ain't necessary."

"No!" Stinky said as others began to look on. "I'll tell you what ain't necessary. It ain't necessary for you to come and try and run my life!"

"I'm not tryin' to run your life, I'm..."

"I'm! I'm what! Every time you see me! That's all you ever talk about and I'm tired of hearin' it! Who's puttin' you up to this, my mother?"

"Come on, Stink, calm down, let's go somewhere and talk, these people are startin' to stare at us."

"These people! These people, are my people! My friends! My partners! My main men, as you call it!"

"Stinky! Come on, man!" Bennett in frustration collared him.

"Get your hands off me! Get off me! Get off me!"

"Everything all right, Stinky?" a fellow who appeared to be blasted out of his mind asked.

"Mind your business!" Bennett said.

"Yeah, I'm cool...*Superstar* here was just leavin'...right?"

Bennett gave Stinky a harsh look just before releasing him. "Yeah, right," he answered dejectedly, and walked away.

"And, don't forget to tell that prima donna, ballerina girlfriend of yours," he jiggled his body jokingly, as a contingent of his friends gathered around him, "that, I said to...hang loose!" The gathering started laughing as Bennett, by this time, started to run.

CHAPTER FIVE

Distressed and mortified, Bennett elected not to show for the New Rochelle game. Kirby did, but he would've been better off staying away. Ironically, Tara was there. She was sitting with Sol and this vivacious blonde. And to top it off, the girl was rooting for New Rochelle. It was a good thing Bennett stayed away.

Mt. Vernon got slaughtered, 104-70. When the game ended, Kirby went into the locker room to talk the incident over with Coach Dee.

Kirby saw him at the water fountain. "Coach Dee!"

"Yeah," Coach answered as he caught a runaway drip of water from his lips, "what do you want?"

"I'm sorry, it was all my fault. He was only tryin' to stop me from gettin' into trouble."

"Yeah, and by doing so, he slit his own wrist."

"What are you talkin' about?" Kirby's heart began to beat rapidly.

Coach Dee stared at him. "That guy you saw me with in that navy suit. He's a rep, from Columbia....Bennett's scholarship is in jeopardy.

"What!"

"I'm having dinner with him tonight at Cromwell's to straighten everything out.

"Oh boy."

"Do me a favor, Kirby. Tell Bennett, I'll call him first thing in the morning to let him know what happened."

The next day came and not a minute too soon. Unusual for that time of year, the weather was sunny and sixty-five degrees. Bennett paced the apartment all morning and finally heard the phone ring.

"Hello!" he said.

"Bennett, this is Coach. Did you talk to Kirby?"

"Yeah, last night."

"Well, here's the situation. You still have your scholarship."

"All right!"

"But," Coach Dee said, "it's on a probationary basis."

"Why probationary?"

"Well, you know, with it being the type of school it is."

Bennett offered a slow smile, "I shouldn't worry since it's only an Ivy League school, right?"

"Right," Coach said, returning the grin he couldn't see. "I wouldn't worry too much, if I were you. You're a good kid. Besides, there's hundreds of other schools."

Bennett regained his confidence, "Thanks, I won't worry."

"So, what are your plans for today?"

"Kirby and I are gonna shoot some baskets, at Fourth Street."

"Now, Bennett. You know how I feel about you guys playing on con..."

"Good-bye, Coach." Bennett hung up.

Bennett and Kirby in their practice uniforms—tube socks, high-top sneakers—were the only people in the park shooting baskets. The others were either standing around conversing or playing handball against the big block of concrete at the center of the park.

A stranger abruptly emerged from the shadows. He was a little on the hairy side, about six feet tall and chubby. Kirby said to himself, Oh no, here comes trouble.

"Ay, young'un," he said to Bennett who was taking chip shots from the foul line. Bennett ignored him and kept shooting. The stranger blocked his shot. He was quick.

"Hey man, you crazy!"

"No, I just want to play. How, about a game?"

"Hey, man, back off. I'm tired."

"Tired from what? You're a young boy."

"Tired from playin' ball, old goat."

Though insulted, the man forced a smile and asked again, "How about a game? Just one...fifty dollars."

"Fifty dollars?" Bennett said as he retrieved the ball and shot again.

"Look, first of all, I don't play for money and second, I don't steal. Playin' you would be grand larceny."

Pleased with his quick comeback, Bennett released a shot that hit nothing but the bottom of the net.

"I'll tell you what. If I win, you owe me nothing. But, if you win, I give you fifty dollars. I just want to play you."

"You're on."

The game started with Bennett taking the ball out and slam-dunking it. That first basket set the stage for his thrashing the man, 32-6.

Gasping for air, the man reached into his sock, pulled out a faded fifty-dollar bill and handed it to Bennett, who had hardly worked up a sweat. "No, man," Bennett said. "I told you, I don't, play for money."

"But, we made a deal. Take it."

"No!" Bennett said and stepped away with his hands up in the air, as if under arrest.

The man put the bill back into his sock. Still reeling from the effects of the beating he took, he panted, "Man, I haven't seen talent like yours in years."

"Is that a fact?"

"Yes, but, please don't think of me as being too old though."

"I hear ya," said Bennett offering his hand in the spirit of sportsmanship. "Thanks. And, you're really not bad yourself."

The two shook hands, and the man left as quickly as he appeared. Kirby said to Bennett while they watched the man leave the park, "Nice guy, huh?"

"Yeah," Bennett answered, not totally convinced. "But, there's somethin' strange about him."

"What do you mean, strange?"

"I don't know. Maybe it's me."

"Well, look on the bright side. At least he wasn't a hustler."

"Yeah, right," Bennett said, watching the man retreat.

"Speakin' of hustler," Kirby said. "You never did tell me how your talk with Stinky went."

"It went nowhere," Bennett answered with sadness. "It went absolutely nowhere. He needs help. Lots and lots of it."

"Well," Kirby said as he snatched the basketball out of Bennett's hands, "if Ms. Robinson wasn't so busy struttin' those big hips all over town, she could help him. Instead she's always 'Bennett, please talk to Stinky, please talk to my baby.' Please this, please that. Stinky's her son, not yours."

"Have some respect. That's his mother. And besides, didn't I help you?"

"I never took that stuff. I was just hangin' out with the pushers, tryin' to pocket a couple of dollars. I wasn't stupid enough to actually get high."

"That's how Stinky started, he wasn't takin' it either, at first."

"Well...I do have respect. But, right is right...And speakin' of those hips," Kirby continued as he emulated the way Ms. Robinson walks. "If she was to ever ask you to..."

"No, Kirby!...No!...Man, you are crazy!" The two broke out into a hearty laugh.

"One more game?" Kirby asked in an attempt to keep the atmosphere light.

"Man, I gotta split. I'm takin' my sweetie to Cromwell's tonight."

"Oh yeah…lookin' like that?"

"What are you talking about?"

"Man, you better head over to Big 3 and get somethin' done to your head first."

"I know, you're right," Bennett said, flashing his trademark smile while running his hand across his uneven hairline. "Dale has probably put out an APB on me."

"Probably."

"Thanks a lot."

"Yeah Ben," Kirby said as he shot another airball, "work hard, get paid, and spend all that money on your lady. Just like a good man should."

"Kirby, you're my boy, but you are one senseless human being."

CHAPTER SIX

Night fell and Bennett with his fresh haircut was dressed sharp as a tack. He had on his new outfit: brown pants, white shirt, brown printed tie, beige jacket and black shoes. He also doused himself with cologne he borrowed from Kirby. He was so emotionally high about the date, he ran all the way to Tara's house, cutting through alleys, dodging traffic and jumping fences. The only thing on his mind was seeing Tara's angelic face.

The second he reached her house, he straightened his tie, rubbed his head and rang the doorbell. Mr. Copeland answered.

"Hello, Bennett."

"Hey, Tim-Tim," he said as he entered.

"Have a seat, my boy. Tara will be down in a minute." Tim-Tim departed to his study. "Tara! Your knight in shining armor is here!"

Not long after, she came down the stairs looking like a princess. Bennett stared at her. His stomach muscles began to rumble and before he could gain control, he let out the loudest belch.

"Hi, ready to go?" Tara said.

Bennett handed her a rose and said, "Just as soon as you are." He then kissed her on the cheek.

"Oh thank you, sweetheart, let me put this in some water."

The couple started for the door when Mr. Copeland entered. "Hey, you two. Going downtown?"

"Yes," they answered.

He approached them with his sweater in hand and said, "Well, I'm going near there. I have to pick up Mrs. Copeland from her bingo. I'll be more than happy to drop you off. That's, of course, if you don't mind?"

"No Daddy, it's okay. We accept."

"Okay, it's settled. Here, Tara, you can start the car."

"I'd better check on Redd. I hear her barking."

The car rode like a dream. It was a dark blue, four-door Pontiac with shiny silver hub caps and white wall tires. Before Bennett knew it, they were nearing the downtown streets of Mt. Vernon. Mr. Copeland broke the silence, "Bennett, my boy, I have a joke for you."

"Oh boy, Tim-Tim, do I have to?"

"Yes, you do…my car, my rules."

"OK," Bennett conceded. "Fire away."

"Well, there's this plane that's about to crash, so the pilot summons a stewardess to ask one of the passengers to say a prayer. She runs down the aisle until she spots an elderly man wearing a hat. She goes over to him and asks, 'Mister, mister, please say a prayer because the plane is about to go down!' He says, 'Hey lady, pardon me, but I haven't been to church in years. I don't really know how to pray.' 'Well,' she says, 'could you at least say a Bible verse or two?' 'Lady,' he answers, 'I haven't picked up a Bible in over twenty years. I couldn't remember a scripture if you paid me.' 'Well,' she says frantically, 'can you at least do *something* religious? Isn't there anything you can do?' The man thought about it for a while then he snapped his fingers, took off his hat, got up and started walking down the aisle. The stewardess said, 'Mister, what are you doing? You're supposed to be doing something religious.' 'I am,' the man replied, 'I'm taking up a collection.'"

Bennett nearly caught cramps in his side from laughing so hard and Tara had tears in her eyes.

Finally after everyone had calmed down, Mr. Copeland asked, "Where are you two going?"

"Cromwell's, Daddy." He whistled, then echoed, "Cromwell's? Pretty nice. This must be a special occasion."

"You know already. Bennett received his scholarship, and we wanted to go somewhere special."

As they pulled up to the restaurant, Mr. Copeland said, "Well, here you are, Cromwell's. Enjoy yourselves. And congratulations, Bennett."

"Thanks, Tim-Tim."

"Thanks, Daddy."

"Tara, don't I get a kiss?" Mr. Copeland asked.

"Yes, Daddy, you do."

"Thank you," Mr. Copeland giggled.

"This place is beautiful," Bennett said as they walked in.

"Yes, it is. Look at those lights hanging from the ceiling...Nice."

"Yeah, I see. They make this carpet look so bright."

"Do you have a reservation, sir?" the maitre d' asked.

"Yes, the name is Wilson. Bennett Wilson." The man checked the reservation book.

"Yes, sir. Right this way, please."

They were led to a table almost in the center of the restaurant. Bennett, feeling something strange, said, "Hey Tara, do you realize we're the only young black couple in here?" She looked at him lovingly, answering, "Yes, and the best part, is that I'm with you."

Bennett smiled, leaned back on his chair and picked up the menu.

"May I take your orders please?" asked the waitress who had long, brown hair and dark brown eyes that twinkled in the light when she smiled.

They ordered the number five: roast beef, fluffy mashed potatoes with melted cheese, green peas, hot buttered rolls and a choice of beverage. Bennett, being health conscious, asked for milk, while Tara ordered orange soda.

The food arrived and went just as fast. They chatted easily.

"So, honey, are you happy about your scholarship?"

"Yeah."

"That's great. I'm so proud of you. So are my parents. Daddy especially, but he won't show it."

"Wait a minute..." Bennett reacted with pleasant surprise. "Your father is proud of me? Tim-Tim?"

"Yes. He told my mother that you'd probably make a great son-in-law."

"Well, will I be his?"

"Bennett, are you trying to propose to me?"

"I just asked a question, that's all."

She began to grin from ear to ear. "Well, that's up to you."

"There you go, Tara, puttin' everything on me. Besides, we're goin' to college."

"So, that doesn't mean we couldn't be married. Remember, I haven't made up my mind about which college I'm going to attend. Columbia, is still on my list."

"Wow," Bennett said looking at the clock on the wall, "it's 11:30. We'd better get outta here."

The check arrived. Bennett reached into his sports jacket for his wallet, and didn't feel anything. He touched his back pocket with the same result. He began to sweat. "I don't have my wallet."

"You what?" Tara asked, as she gasped at the $21.50 bill.

"I don't have my wallet! I forgot it!"

The waitress, seeing how fidgety Bennett was, sensed something was wrong and came over. "Is there a problem?"

Before Bennett could respond, Tara smiled, "No." She pulled two tens and a five from her purse, and gave it to the waitress, and told her, "Keep the change."

Bennett, feeling like his manhood was lost, got up and stormed out in disgust, leaving a trail of dust behind. "I'm so stupid," he said, "I was so excited about finally bein' able to go to a decent restaurant and I leave my wallet home."

Tara put her arms around him, stood on her toes and gave him a kiss that sent shock waves through his body.

"Honey," Tara attempted to placate Bennett, "you're not stupid. Aside from feeling bad for you, I feel good 'cause you're so excited. If you only knew how good that makes me feel, you wouldn't feel bad."

"I love you, Tara. I love you so much!"

"Oh, baby, I love you, too."

Tara gave Bennett a wink and said, "Let's go to my house, my parents should be asleep by now."

CHAPTER SEVEN

"Hey, Bennett, you eatin' this mess?" Kirby asked pointing to his tray.

"Not me, man. Every time, I come in here, I get the creeps."

"I-I-I d-d-d…"

"Come on, big fella, let it out, you can do it!" Kirby yelled to Big Joe, who was slapping on the table and stomping his feet trying to get the words out.

The prefix "big" in Joe's name was an understatement. The guy was a man-child. Not only was he tall—six-feet-eight—he was heavy too. He wore an Afro with side burns, a goatee and mustache. His walk was peculiar looking, for he was somewhat hunchback and he had a gallop to his strut.

"Stop Kirby," Bennett commanded. "Let him speak."

"But…he ain't sayin' anything!" Kirby said and gave Big Joe and incredulous look. "I don't understand 'd-d-d'!"

"D-D-Don't c-c-care 'b-b-bout y-y-you two, 'cause I'm g-g-gonna eat."

"Y-Y-You eat anything," Kirby said.

"Sh-Sh-Shut up, s-s-swamprrrat, b-b-before I t-t-take y-y-your h-h-head off."

When Bennett interrupted, "Be nice ladies," the guys broke out into laughter. He then added, "Kirby, one of these days Joe's gonna get you."

All of a sudden there was a louder noise.

"I'm butt naked!" Stinky screamed from the top of a table. The scream was thunderous. And when he jumped down and started running around, the cafeteria went wild. The girls panted in surprise and shock. Some of the guys snickered while others looked on in disbelief. Stinky was dodging monitors, knocking over tables, pushing students to the floor, and going absolutely berserk. After nearly ten minutes of trying, the monitors finally caught him, wrapped him in a coat and escorted him out.

In the locker room that day before practice all you heard was chuckling over Stinky's performance. Neither Bennett nor Kirby found it very amusing. Bennett was so upset that he didn't want to practice, but he did.

After practice, Kirby tried to cheer him up. "Hey, Bennett, a hookshot from half court, the loser picks up the tab at Fancy's."

Fancy's was their favorite after-practice hangout.

Kirby missed on four tries. Bennett made his first with ease.

"Come on, Kirb, let's get dressed and get outta here."

Bennett threw up his last shot...nothing but the bottom of the net.

"Oh, man, it's rainin' cats and dogs out here."

"And, you have to work tonight?"

"Tonight! Forget it. I have to be at work as soon as possible. One of our guys is on vacation, so the rest of us have to work extra hours."

"Extra hours, extra money."

"You know it." The two gents exchanged fives.

Kirby added, "Try and keep your mind off Stinky."

"Yeah, I'll try. You owe me a burger," Bennett added as he ran off.

"Ay, Bennett, take my umbrella!"

"I don't need it!"

"You, dummy," Kirby mumbled to himself as he watched him race down the street.

CHAPTER EIGHT

"Hey, Bennett."

"Hey, Marge, what's up?"

Marge was a waitress and definitely not the type of girl you bring home to Momma.

"The sky, Bennett! What else would be up?"

"What about this, Marge?" Her eyes followed Bennett's hands.

"Watch it, Bennett!" Bill walked toward them.

"I was only playin'," Bennett said.

"Yeah, but this is a place of business, not pleasure," Bill said. "Now, let's get to work."

"See ya, Marge."

While downstairs changing, Bennett said aloud to himself, "Bill must've climbed down the wrong side of his tree this mornin'."

Bennett was tired. The practice, the episode over Stinky, the weather, and the dash to work had gotten the better of him. So he decided to lie down for what he figured would be a ten minute nap. Comfortable in the fresh and well-furnished changing quarters, he fell asleep for what turned into two hours.

The crowd was large for a rainy night, and he wasn't missed. That was until Bill noticed the floor was extremely wet, dirty and slippery. Bill shouted Bennett's name across the restaurant.

"I haven't seen him," Marge said, unaware of what was going on.

"Where is he?" Bill said angrily and stormed downstairs.

"Wake up!" Bill shouted, rousing Bennett. "Wake up! You're not home."

"Oh, sorry, Bill," Bennett yawned and rubbed sleep from his eyes.

"Bennett, if you can't hack this job, then quit, but don't come here to sleep. This is the third time in two weeks. One more time and you're fired! Do you understand?"

"Yeah, I understand."

"And for sleeping, you'll stay an extra hour, after closin'."

Bill made his way back upstairs with a sleepy and chagrined Bennett behind him.

Bennett worked and worked and worked. The time slipped by before he knew it. "Bill, what time is it?"

"It's a quarter after three."

"Three-fifteen? Bill, I'm in bed sleepin' by this time."

"Stick around a few minutes," Bill said. "I'll give you a ride."

"If you let me go now, I can run home."

"Run home? You're nuts, it's pouring out there for God's sake."

"I just want to go home."

He arrived home a wet, weary young man only to find Yvette sitting at the kitchen table sobbing. Alarmed, he said, "Where's Momma and Champ? They all right?"

"Yeah, they're fine."

"Well, why are you cryin'?" Bennett said, still shakened.

"It's Stinky," she said while trying to gather herself. "He jumped out the window and killed himself."

"What?" Bennett said in disbelief. "When?"

"Round nine," she said, still sobbing.

"How come no one came to get me?" Bennett said, overcome with emotion. "Man, if only I could've been there," he continued as he dragged his wet and tired body toward the couch where he dropped himself in a dead heap and lay his head back and allowed the tears which had begun to fill his eyes to run down his face. "I should've been there, Yvette. I should've been there. He wouldn't have…he couldn't have done it, if I was there. Man!"

"You can't blame yourself. You didn't have anything to do with it. He was a junkie, and you know, you did all you could to help him."

Bennett realized she was right. "I'm going over there."

"Momma's there. Why don't you stay home and rest?"

"No, I'm going over there, now."

After pulling himself together and regaining his composure, Bennett was off again.

⚜

"Ms. Robinson, I know this may not help much, but if you need a son, I'll gladly volunteer. I can find time to help you around here some."

Ms. Robinson replied with a hug, "You're so sweet. You've done enough, and in time, I'll be fine. God bless you." Bennett's mother was filled with pride.

Up all night, Bennett decided to go home, skip school and get some rest. There was a game later that day.

While sleeping, he dreamt a terrifying dream. He was in a classroom dead, lying in a black coffin with blood trickling down his face. He realized he was having a nightmare, so he attempted to pry open his eyes. But when he tried, his old fifth-grade teacher, Ms. Becker, appeared, tapping her pointer stick against the blackboard under the word *Bennett*. The dream scared him so much he was afraid to get out of bed when he finally awakened.

He arrived at school within minutes of the game and was a total wreck.

"Ay Bennett," Kirby said, "were you able to get any sleep? I know it must've been tough on you. Believe it or not, it was tough on me too."

"Yeah," Bennett answered shaking his head and opening his locker.

Kirby walked over to him and placed his hand on Bennett's shoulder, "Are you gonna be okay, man?"

"No, Kirb," Bennett shook his head again. "It's me. I don't know, I had this wild dream."

"Aw, we all have those," Kirby said, waving his hand.

"But, not like this one. I was dead."

"Come on, Bennett. Man, it was only a nightmare, a dream."

"No, it was real. I saw my face," Bennett said pointing to himself.

"Bennett, Stinky just died, remember? You were probably dreamin' about him and saw your face, that's all."

Bennett said with fright in his voice, "I'm not gonna see my next birthday."

"Are you crazy? You ain't gonna die no time soon. You're young still. Young and strong...and ugly."

"Stop kiddin' around, and who are you to say I won't die?"

"It was just a dream, just a dream. Come on, pull yourself together."

"I don't know, Kirb. And why couldn't the school or Coach at least try to postpone the game? I mean..."

"Look Bennett, it ain't like he was currently playin' or anything. He wasn't even in school. They released a sympathy statement, but they won't give what he did much respect. Cancelin' a game, for him? He was a druggie and a drop out. Streakin' in the lunch room, I mean, come on Bennett."

"So! What should that mean? He was human, and he was still once a part of this team. Shoot…he was the only guy that ever beat me one on one."

"Well, I don't know. But I do know this. He taught me that when I die, I wanna die with some dignity. I ain't about bein' drugged up, hallucinatin' and thinkin' I could fly. I ain't lookin' for nobody to name no streets and stuff after me when I go, but at least give me some kinda respect. And as for you, you stop worryin' about him. His funeral is Monday, and you stop tryin to die off, too. In your heart just dedicate this game and the rest of the season to him. You did all you could do."

Kirby finally got through to him.

"Now, come on, get dressed, cause we got a playoff spot to clinch. I'll meet you downstairs. Hurry up, man."

The gym was packed and the intensity level was high as always. The game started with Bennett receiving the jumpball tap from Big Joe, racing down court, jumping at the foul line, floating through the air and jamming home a slam dunk. The dunk sent the crowd into orbit. Kirby didn't know for sure, but it seemed like his talk had put some kind of magical spell on Bennett. He broke "Gusta's" game point record of 52 set in 1957, by scoring 59 points in their 101-87 drubbing of Rice High School.

"Gusta," short for Gus Tatum, was the master of the two hand set shot. He was known as a pure shooter and trick shot artist. He was also a renowned gambling man. In fact, legend has it that he once bet a fellow classmate that he could sink a ninety-foot over-head shot backwards; the loser had to walk the halls for one period quacking like a duck...stark naked. "Gusta" won the bet. The classmate, like Stinky, was taken into custody.

They started for the locker room in the usual broken-line formation. Bennett was a few players in front of Kirby when he saw the man he didn't care for approach and drop a roll of bills at his feet.

"My man," Bennett said, "you dropped your cash."

"This is yours, Blood. I told you before. If you lost your next game, you'd get rich. Didn't I?"

"*I* didn't lose the last game. *We* lost 'cause I got suspended and didn't play. That's all."

The man pulled him aside.

"Say, it's a bit too crowded in here. Get dressed and meet me outside."

"For what?" Bennett said as the man picked up his loot.

"Look, Blood," the man said backing away, "I told you it's too crowded, so meet me outside," he said while pointing toward an exit.

Bennett stared at him momentarily, then remembered Tara was in the bleachers with Dannon and Yvette.

"Tara, take them home. I'll be there in a little while!"

Bennett then turned and headed for the locker room.

Kirby was dressed in his street clothes when Bennett arrived. "Yo, Bennett, please stay away from that guy. You see what just happened to Stinky."

"I know, Kirb, I'm just gonna see what he wants...that's all. Besides, maybe I can find out what really happened."

"You know what happened. You know what he wants, so stay away."

Bennett proceeded to get dressed. "Thanks, Kirb, but I'm not gettin' into anything I shouldn't be. You know me."

Kirby believed him. But there was something about the way Bennett answered that made him uneasy.

He went over to Big Joe's locker. "Big-man, we're gonna have to keep a real close eye on Bennett. Either that or break Rooster Hat's neck!"

"P-P-P..."

"Take your time, Joe," Kirby said.

"P-P-Personally," Big Joe began to pound his feet against the floor, "I v-v-vote f-f-for the la-la-latter."

While standing near Big Joe, Kirby thought, Coach can't find out about this. He knew how important it was to keep it to himself.

About the same time, Bennett was walking through the dark, vacant parking lot when he heard, "It's about time, Youngblood."

"I'm here, ain't I?"

Out of nowhere, a car door swung open, "Get in."

Bennett stood motionless amidst the cool dark night, "Where are we going?"

"Don't worry, I won't hurt you. Besides, if I did, I'm sure you have friends. Now come on."

"I'm not worried 'bout you hurtin' me."

"Blood, my name is Simon," Simon said after shaking hands with Bennett. "Simon Diamond. And my driver's name is Willie.

Relax, we just want to talk, is all. Here, some smoke." He offered Bennett a joint.

"How could you offer me that junk after what just happened to my man Stinky?"

"Hey," Simon said innocently, "I know he was your boy, but he was trippin' long before he met me. I didn't have anything to do with him wantin' to walk on air. He was a dust head."

"Is that your real name?" Bennett tried to change the subject.

"Of course not."

"What is it then?"

Simon began fanning himself with dollar bills while he continued to puff on his marijuana.

"That I won't tell you until we get better acquainted."

They drove around for a while before pulling up in front of Bennett's building. Simon fixed his hat and sat back and folded his arms. "Youngblood, I won't procrastinate any longer. I have a serious proposition for you."

Bennett let down the window, relieving himself from the contact high. "What kind of proposition?"

"You can have all of this if you play ball with me."

"I play ball for, and with, Mt. Vernon." Bennett snatched at the handle. The door was locked and the engine was off. Bennett whirled around and looked at Diamond. "What do you want with me?"

"Just listen to me, that's all. Listen for two minutes."

Bennett had no choice, "Okay, Diamond, it's your nickel. You got two minutes."

"I hear ya, Youngblood," Simon said, again flashing the roll of bills. "This can be all yours—all you have to do is throw your next game against New Ro'."

"No, no way, Diamond! Now, open the door!"

"Listen first. You told me you'd listen. Besides, I still have a minute, fifty seconds."

Bennett took a deep breath and let it out slowly.

Simon continued. "Now, for the New Ro' game. The odds are five to one, Mt. Vernon. But me and my establishment will bet against them."

"That's your establishment's problem."

"Come on, man, lighten up. All I'm sayin' is throw one game, one lousy game. You only lost three and you're in the playoffs."

"So!"

"Not only that, but see what you pass up? Hundreds and hundreds. This right here is at least three months' rent."

"Three months' rent?"

"Three months' rent, maybe more, Youngblood."

"Look, I don't know."

"Tell you what, Youngblood, think about it over the weekend. If you throw it, this is yours. This is double what you would've gotten before 'cause you've already made me a lot of money with Mt. Vernon losing that last game."

Willie started the car, unlocked the door and pulled off as Bennett stepped out. He stood on the sidewalk confused amid car exhaust fumes.

Tara was upstairs, furious.

"Mr. Wilson, where were you?"

He looked at her with a who-do-you-think-you-are expression and didn't answer.

"Where were you?" Tara repeated. Bennett collected his coolness.

"Look, Tara, a friend invited me out. Don't worry, it was a male." Laughing, he bent over and they kissed.

"I love you," he said.

Tara's anger was obliterated by Bennett's sweet diplomacy. "Do you want me to fix you something to eat or have you already eaten…with your friend?"

"No, that's all right, I'll grab somethin' at Dex's party."

"Party! The one you know I don't want you to go to!"

"Yeah, but…"

"Bennett, that isn't fair."

"Fair?"

"That's right. Why can't you spend your night off with me?"

"I told them I'd be there. It's in Stinky's honor."

"That junkie's dead!" she said venomously.

He gave her a look that needed no words.

Realizing that was the wrong thing to say, Tara went over to his chair in the sparsely furnished living room. "I'm sorry, but lately it seems like you've been neglecting me. Don't you love me anymore?"

"Of course I do."

Tara figured he'd cave in, now that she had him where she wanted him. "Are you still going to the party?"

"Yes, love."

"Love? You don't love me!"

"Tara," he grabbed her. "I have a few things on my mind. I'm just gonna go be with the fellas, that's all. Hey, you can come if you want. You're invited too!"

"Get your hands off me!" She yanked away and started for the door with coat in hand.

"You forgot your car keys," Bennett said.

Tara turned, snatched her keys and said, "Thank you," and slammed the door, all in one swift motion.

"Who slammed the door?" Yvette yelled.

"Nobody. Go to sleep."

Dexter shared his house with his two older brothers, Derrick and Dannie-boy. It was a gray, rundown two-story that leaned to the side.

"Hey, Ben," Dexter greeted Bennett at the door.

"Ay, Dex, I'm here."

"Ben-Ben, I thought you wasn't gonna make it for a little while...I was gettin' kinda worried there."

"I told you I'd make it, didn't I?"

"Yeah," Dexter said as he was looking over Bennett's shoulder. "Hey, where's Tara?"

"You can stop lookin'. She isn't comin'."

"Why?"

Bennett waved him off, "long story."

"Sounds like you been fightin' to me," Dexter said curiously.

"Nothin' serious," Bennett walked into the house.

Surprisingly, the inside of the house was quite nice, with finely crafted art adorning the walls, family photos spread about the house, and swinging doors separating every room.

Kirby spotted Bennett over by the fireplace with a puzzled look on his face.

"Ay, Bennett, what's up?"

"What?"

"Bennett, did you hear what I said?"

"No, what did you say?"

"Never mind." Kirby's attention was navigated elsewhere. "OOOHH, OOOHH."

"What's up?" Bennett asked.

"Look at Angela. Shucks! I didn't know honor students could look like that. Those legs are kickin'. Yes, indeed!"

"Hi Bennett." Kathy joined the two, "Where's Tara?"

"Home, I guess."

"Oh, that's too bad," Kathy said and looked at Kirby. Kathy was a tall and sophisticated young lady, very pretty. Being part Native American—her grandmother was full-blooded Cherokee—she had long, slick, jet black hair, and her skin was a rich coffee color that blended perfectly with her eyes. Kirby knew his Kathy wasn't as endowed as Angela, but he also knew she was no slouch either.

"May I have this dance my handsome man?...Kirby...Kirby!"

"Yes! Yes! Yes! Oh Yes!, you may, my beautiful lady. Hold this Bennett."

"Man, Kirby, this is terrible."

"I know, I spiked it."

"With what, turpentine?"

"No, root beer," Kirby said with a smile and took off with Kathy.

Just before the dance, the dee jay announced that the next song would be played not only in honor of Stinky, but for all of the victims of the Vietnam War. Slow dancing with his lady to the smooth sound of "What's Goin' On" by Marvin Gaye, Kirby watched Angela make her way through the crowd and approach Bennett.

When they stopped dancing, Kirby said to Kathy, "What would Tara do if she happened to walk in?" But since he saw they were just talking, they resumed. A few minutes later, Kirby checked again. They were dancing. "Hold on, baby. Let me go see if I can talk some sense into Bennett."

When he got to Bennett he tapped him on the shoulder. "Yo, you better be cool. What if Tara decides to come?"

"Leave me alone. I know what I'm doin'!"

"Yeah, leave him alone," Angela added.

"Okay, it's your funeral."

Kirby started back to Kathy on the other side of the dance floor. As he stopped between couples, he had a sudden urge to look back. And who should be coming through the door with a warm and friendly smile on her face?

"Bennett, look out!" The music was too loud. Bennett didn't hear Kirby.

While Tara was peering over and around couples, Kirby figured he'd have just enough time to reach Bennett. But he didn't. The very second Tara spotted Bennett, Angela made eye contact with her and planted a kiss on his cheek. Tara stormed over so fast you would've thought her pants were on fire.

"I hate you, Bennett Wilson! I hate you!" Tara screamed after she reached up and slugged him. Bennett actually staggered, the hit was that hard.

He held his cheek, in shock and surprise, hearing bells ringing in his ears.

"Hey, girl! What's your problem!" Angela said.

"You better shut up, girl, before I slap you, too." Tara stormed off.

"Let her go," Kirby said. "Once she cools off, she'll be all right."

"Yeah, you're right. But, I don't know what's been happenin' to me lately. I just don't know."

"Bennett," Kirby said, putting his hand on his shoulder, "don't forget you had trouble on your job. Stinky smoked angel dust and thought he was Superman and killed himself, and you almost got your scholarship taken away. That's a lot of pressure for anyone to deal with, in such a short time. Shucks! Even over a long time it's a lot."

"I guess you're right."

"I know I am, so stick around a while and enjoy yourself. But watch your back," Kirby said with a smile.

"Be cool Kirby. But I'll be headin' home now. I gotta go to work tomorrow."

"I'll get Kathy and we'll leave together."

"No. There's no sense in you havin' a short evenin' on my account. Stay...for my sake."

"Okay, I'll stay. But only because you're tellin' me to stay."

Bennett gave Kirby a firm pat on the back that made him cough.

"My man," he said.

"So I'll see you, tomorrow, after you get off."

"No, not tomorrow. Tomorrow's Dannon's birthday. I'm takin' him out somewhere."

"Okay then. I'll see you at the funeral."

Before Kirby knew it, Bennett was out the door.

CHAPTER NINE

"Wake up, Champ," Bennett said, kneeling at Dannon's bedside. "Wake up. It's your birthday."

Dannon rubbed his eyes. "Hi, Big Bra. Where's Momma?"

"She's in bed sleepin'. She's tired from work last night."

"But, she was supposed to make my birthday breakfast. She always makes it."

"Shh, Dannon. Don't wake up Yvette."

"I'm not sleep," Yvette said and sat up. "Dannon, Momma's too tired. I'm makin' you breakfast."

"Yuck! Phooey!"

"Stop that, Dannon," Bennett admonished. "Now, tell me where you want to go today?"

Quickly forgetting about his birthday breakfast, Dannon said cheerfully, "To the circus! Big Bra, can we go to the circus?"

"The circus, Champ?"

"Yeah!"

"Okay, the circus it is."

"Is Tara coming too?"

"No Champ, I'm afraid not, we had a little fight."

"You punched her?"

"No," Bennett said rubbing the left side of his face. "I wouldn't hit Tara."

"I want her to come with us, Big Bra. I like her."

"I do, too, but, I don't know. Look, Champ," Bennett said, "you just be ready when I get home."

"Okay."

"And as for you, pumpkin," Bennett took hold of Yvette, "when your birthday comes in October, I'll do the same for you. I promise."

Bennett picked up his little sister and kissed her on the forehead.

"Okay, Bennett, but I don't want to go to the circus."

"No problem," Bennett said. "Hey, I better get outta here if I don't want to be late."

He stepped out of the room. "Man, I sure wish I had a real bed. That sofa ain't doing much for my back."

All morning Tara monopolized Bennett's thoughts. While Bennett was on his lunch break, he decided to call her to patch things up.

"Hello," a strange voice answered.

"Who's this!"

"This is Sol, who's this?"

"You creep! What are you doin' over there, and where's Tara?"

"Sh-sh-she's in the kitchen. D-d-do you wa-wa-want her?"

"What do you think?"

"Hello," Tara said in a sweet and mellow voice.

"Hello, nothin'! What's he doin' there?"

"We're studying for a biology exam. And why all the hostility, Bennett? It wasn't me slow dancing with a hussy last night, was it? How did she feel?"

"Tara, look..."

"Bennett, I was hurt and embarrassed."

"Embarrassed? Tara, I'm sorry. Besides, you have Mr. Green Eyes answerin' the telephone."

"Goodbye, Bennett!"

Before Bennett could respond, his ear was buzzing from a hostile dial tone.

"Well, you've done it now," Bennett said aloud to himself.

Bill approached him as he was hanging up. "Fightin' with your old lady?"

"Yeah," Bennett said solemnly, with his head facing down. "Bill, can I punch back in now?"

"We can handle it. Besides, you have a half hour yet."

"I know, but still."

"Okay. It's your lunch break."

Bennett went downstairs. "How in the world am I gonna enjoy myself with Dannon with all this on my mind?"

In a daze all the way home, his key was in the door before he knew it.

"Dannon, you ready yet?"

"He's not here, Bennett. I sent him downstairs to get a cup of sugar from Lois," his mother said from the kitchen.

Kirby's mother, Lois, and Mrs. Wilson were as close as Bennett and Kirby. In fact, Kirby's mother helped Mrs. Wilson get her job. The shop steward was an old friend.

"Momma," Bennett said, "what are you doin' home?"

"I felt sick so I stayed home."

Bennett felt a real sharp pain in the pit of his stomach.

"Momma, why you still gettin' sick?"

"I don't know, son, but the good Lord is carryin' me through. I know that."

"Yes, Momma, I know," Bennett said and embraced her.

"But, let me quit school for a little while. I'll see if I can get day hours at Hamburger Haven and get a second job at night."

"No! Now we've been through this before."

"But, Momma..."

"Look, son, school is important. Very important. I wasn't so lucky when I was comin' up. My daddy made me and Daisy quit school to get jobs when we were in the ninth and tenth grades. You see how she turned out, don't you? Son, I love you for what you're tryin' to do. But, the Lord will see us through, just hold on. Besides, baby, with this war goin' on, you're liable to get drafted if you drop out. I don't want to take no chance on losing you to no war."

"Well…maybe I shouldn't spend money today on Dannon," Bennett said.

"Now, Bennett, that's gonna hurt him. It's bad enough I couldn't get him nothin' but a poster of…what's that basketball player's name?"

"Dr. J."

"Yeah, him! So, don't worry. You're all the daddy he's got now since your father walked out on us. So enjoy yourselves. Besides, baby, Stinky's funeral is in a few days and you need to ease your mind…go."

"But, Momma…"

"You heard me," Mrs. Wilson said. "When Dannon comes back, tell him to put the sugar in the Kool-Aid and take his medicine. I'll see you both later. Have a good time."

"Hey, Champ, you ready yet?" Bennett asked as Dannon opened the door.

"Yeah, but first let me see if Momma wants me to do somethin'.'"

"Wait, Momma told me."

Dannon took his medicine, and exploded into the room for his jacket. "Big Bra! How, are we gettin' there?"

"The iron horse," Bennett answered in between sips of Kool-Aid.

"The train?"

"Yeah! The train! What other kind of horse did you think I was talkin' about…Trigger…Mr. Ed?"

"How far is Madison Square Garden?" Dannon asked as he approached Bennett near the door.

"It's on 34th Street, and we'll be gettin' on the number two train at 241st Street. It's about twenty-nine stops, at an average of a minute and a half between each. So you figure, close to forty-five minutes."

"Oh goodie, a long time on the train."

"Oh boy."

CHAPTER TEN

"Hurry up! The show is about to start," Bennett said while posing in the mirror of the Garden bathroom.

"Okay, I'm comin'!"

"You should've told me you were feelin' nauseous before we left home. Those poor women. You threw up all over them."

"I'm finished now." Dannon was fastening his zipper.

"If I'd known you were gonna get sick, I wouldn't have taken off work three hours early," Bennett complained as they left the bathroom.

Dannon was saddened, "I'm sorry, Big Bra."

They left the men's room and walked the crowded corridor of the Madison Square Garden. In a matter of minutes they had reached their seats.

"Hot dogs! Hot dogs! Get your delicious hot dogs! Hot dogs here!" shouted the hot dog vendor with the red and white striped jacket.

"Big Bra, I want a hot dog," Dannon said as they watched the animals enter the ring.

"A hot dog?"

"Yeah, I'm hungry!"

"But, you just finished throwin' up and you want a hot dog?"

"Yeah!"

"Okay," Bennett sighed, "call the man."

"Hot dog here! Get your delicious hot dogs here!"

"Over here, mister!" Dannon said.

"Whadda ya have, one, two, three or four?"

"I'll have one."

"Make that two," Bennett corrected.

"Mustard or relish?"

"Both," Dannon said.

"Okay, fellas, here ya go. That'll be one dollar, please."

"Thank you," Dannon said. "Big Bra, that guy is the same color as these hot dogs." The hot dog man was serving another person down the aisle.

"That ain't nice," Bennett said with a smile.

"I know, but he is. Hey, look at what the elephant over there is doin'!"

"Come on, not while I'm eatin'!"

Dannon started laughing. "What's wrong? Does that remind you of somethin'?"

"Who told you about that?"

"Tara," Dannon said still laughing.

"Okay, now shut up, clown, and watch the circus."

The circus at Madison Square Garden had been a tradition for many years. Every show was standing room only. And with just enough room to breathe, and depending on where you sat, you could barely see without stretching your neck.

All in all, Bennett was satisfied because Dannon had an absolute ball. But, after all of the hilarious high jinx the circus had to offer, it was time to go home.

The instant Dannon boarded the subway, he went out like a light. Before Bennett knew it, he too was in a deep sleep.

"Who is it?" Yvette said frightened to death by the pounding on the door.

"It's me, Bennett."

"Well, don't bang the door down," Yvette ordered as she looked through the peep hole.

"Where's your key?"

"Open the door, Yvette! Champ weighs a ton."

"Did you have fun?"

"Yeah, we did," Bennett said chuckling. "Especially after he threw up all over three old ladies."

As he laid the fully dressed Dannon on the bed, he heard Yvette's puzzled, "What?"

Bennett began unlacing Dannon's sneakers. "Yep, just what I said."

"Ill!"

"What are you illin' about? You threw up on people when you were smaller."

"I did?"

"Momma home?" Bennett quickly changed the subject.

"No, she went over to Ms. Robinson's."

"Oh, she's feelin' better?"

"Thank God," Yvette said. "Where are you goin'?"

"To Aunt Daisy's house."

"Oh, Tara called. She..."

"Who cares?" Bennett said and left the apartment with nothing but Tara on his mind.

CHAPTER ELEVEN

"Quiet! Quiet! Quiet!" Mr. Whitby shouted to the class while tapping his pointer on his desk. "This is a classroom, not a ballroom. I demand quiet in my classroom. The grades scored on last week's test were just horrible. It's a shame only five of twenty of you passed!" Mr. Whitby was not in one of his better moods. "And you, Mr. Wilson," Whitby said to an inattentive Bennett, "I'm surprised at you. You're one of my best students."

"Mr. Whitby, hey, I'm sorry, if I fouled up the test."

"Never mind the apologies. In fact, I'd like to see you after class."

Bennett didn't respond. His thoughts were of Stinky's funeral the day before and how his classmates were still acting as if nothing ever happened.

Kirby, seeing the despondent look on Bennett's face, tapped him on the arm. "Lighten up, man. Again, you have to realize, society frowns upon Stinky's kind of folk."

"*Society*," Bennett sighed. "But, he was so young...our age."

"Look, you did what most people wouldn't do. You tried to help, and that's all you can ask."

"Yeah, I suppose you're right."

While Bennett was still in a fog, Tara walked in.

"Where were you, young lady?" Mr. Whitby asked.

"I had to go to the ladies' room."

"That's no excuse. You're still late. You should've come here first, then asked to be excused."

"Well, I'm sorry, Mr. Whitby," Tara said with a bit of annoyance.

"Just be seated, young lady."

Bennett's expression indicated that he wasn't too thrilled by the way she was treated. Several minutes passed, when Angela walked in.

"Where were you, Angela?" Mr. Whitby spoke ever so calmly.

"My locker was jammed, so I waited for the custodian."

"Quiet!" Mr. Whitby said. "What are you people grumbling about?"

Ten minutes later came the third interruption of the day. It was Miss Peacock, the Chemistry II teacher from down the hall. Miss Peacock was unfortunate. Because, if there was ever a person whose name bore witness of the way the person looked...she was it.

"I want your Benedict's Solution," Miss Peacock snapped. Mr. Whitby snapped back.

"No, you can't have my solution. But, you can have an invitation to your own classroom." Whitby pointed toward the door. "In other words...Disappear!"

"OOOHH, OOOHH, OOOHH!" the class mocked in unison.

"Well, I never!" she said and stomped out.

"I know it!"

The class bellowed with laughter. Miss Peacock stepped back in.

"Why you, callow, myopic...you charlatan!"

"OOOHH, OOOHH, OOOHH!"

"Okay, class, let's knock it off, let's knock it off...the virago is gone."

It was the end of the fifth period and the bell didn't ring a second too soon.

"Wilson, don't leave. I want to see you."

"Yo, Kirby, I'll meet you in the lunchroom."

All of the students cleared the classroom except Bennett, who stood by Mr. Whitby's desk and Angela, who remained in her seat.

"I'd like to know what the problem is concerning your grades. It seems ever since you received the scholarship, you've simply gone downward. What's the problem? Tell me."

With thoughts of Tara on his mind, Bennett said, "Well, Mr. Whitby, with all due respect, it's none of your business."

"I'm only trying to help."

"Help? How? By usin' that tone of voice?"

"Now, look, Wilson."

"No, you look. First, of all, my mother is very sick. Her blood pressure is sky high. I come to school from eight to three, I play ball from four to seven, I have a job and work from eight to two in the mornin', sometimes three, dependin' if I'm caught sleepin'."

"But, I'm..."

"Don't even try it because I don't want to hear it. The next time, a student is havin' a problem, ask nicely and you might learn somethin'. Good day, Mr. Whitby...Angela."

❧⦿❧

"Yo, Bennett, over here!" Kirby shouted from the snack bar line.

"Yeah Kirb, what's up?"

"You tell me, Ben-Ben. What went down with you and Whitby?"

"That old crab made me mad."

"Because of Tara?" Kirby said laughing.

"No, of course not. He just got on my case for no real reason, that's all."

"Bennett, where's your books? I didn't do my English home-work last night."

"Oh, I left them in Whitby's. I'll be right back."

"I'll hold your place!"

Bennett dashed back to Whitby's and without breaking momentum opened the classroom door.

"Whoa! Whoa! What in the…! Yo! Yo! Mr. Whitby! What are you doin' to Angela?"

"What are you doing barging into my classroom!"

"I forgot my books," Bennett said, pleading innocent. But in an attempt to rub things in, he added, "Hey, I'll get right out of your way."

"Yeah, you do that," Angela shot back while fastening her buttons.

As Bennett strolled the hall en route to the lunchroom, he couldn't help but repeat to himself what he had just seen. *Whitby messin' with Angela.*

"Ben-Ben, what's that look, man?"

Bennett, looking like he was having a pleasant dream said, "Nothin' Kirb, nothin', at all."

Kirby didn't believe him.

"I still need your English book."

"Yo, Kirb, see you at practice."

⁓◉⁓

Bennett was awesome that day. His aerial assaults were breathtaking. So much so, his teammates—those who were supposed to be his scrimmage opponents—didn't want to check him.

From the foul line, he went. From the left side, he went. Down the middle, he went. It was a sight.

Coach Dee had that look—I'm sure glad he's on our side.

Bennett and Kirby stayed after practice. Bennett took foul shots and Kirby retrieved.

"Say, Bennett," Kirby said in an attempt to divert his mind from the popping sound of the net, "ya hear from Tara lately?"

"Naw, man," he answered not breaking his rhythm.

"Bennett, I have a confession to make." The popping of the net was Bennett's only response. "It's about Tara."

His concentration finally broke. "What about her?"

The ball rolled down the court.

"Well," Kirby said backing away. "I sorta called her that Friday. That Friday you stepped…"

"You what!"

"I'm sorry," Kirby said as a strange look came over Bennett.

"Sorry, for what? We don't go together anymore."

"I know, but…"

"Aw, forget it."

Kirby felt relieved, to the point where he had enough nerve to challenge Bennett to another trick shot bet. He missed as usual on all five tries and like always, Bennett made his on the first.

"Put it on my tab, Mr. Wilson," Kirby said, knowing he didn't have a dime.

"Yeah, right. Let's hit the showers."

"Hey, Joe, what are you doin' tonight?" Kirby asked while posing in the mirror.

"N-N-Nothin', K-K-Kirb, I h-h-have an exam t-t…."

"Tomorrow…Solid."

"W-W-Why are y-y-you s-s-so d-d-dressed up?"

"I-I-I g-g-got somewhere to go tonight."

"What's that smell?" Bennett said sniffing a peculiar scent.

"Yeah, I s-s-smell it t-t-too."

"F-F-For y-y-your in-in-information ladies, it's my new cologne," Kirby said.

"What's it called? 'Kill a deadman'?" Bennett cracked, and in jest he and Big Joe slapped five.

"No, it's English Leather," Kirby answered.

"N-N-No w-w-way, Jose." Big Joe countered, "I have E-E-English L-L-Leather, and it d-d-don't s-s-smell l-l-like th-th-that."

"I-I-I know. I mixed it with somethin'."

"With what?" Bennett said, holding his nose. "Man, that stuff smells like feet!"

"N-N-None of your business."

"Let's get him!" Bennett motioned to Big Joe. Kirby's eyes popped open when he saw the two giants coming at him. He ran to his right, and straight into Bennett. He ran to his left and smack into Big Joe. He fell to his knees and cried playfully. The two bullies picked him up like a baby and carried him to the showers. The second Kirby noticed where they were taking him, he started kicking and screaming for dear life. To no avail. He was thrown into the showers, cologne and all—with the members of the wrestling team. Everyone was laughing at him while he was getting drenched.

"Big Joe! Bennett! I'll get you back for this!"

While in the shower getting soaked, Kirby was offered a bar of soap, by a wrestler. Kirby wanted to make him eat it, but he was so huge he could've eaten him.

⌘

"Hey, Bennett, did you hear the news?" Kirby said. They were at Bennett's locker just before first period the next day.

"No, bud, what's up?"

"Somehow, word got back to school officials that Whitby and Angela were foolin' around in his classroom. He was fired and she was kicked out of the Honor Society."

"Oh yeah!" Bennett said as if someone had died.

"What's wrong?"

"Nothin'." His voice cracked. But I didn't tell anybody—I didn't tell a soul, he thought to himself.

Bennett was strolling down the student-filled hallway when Angela approached him.

"Bennett Wilson! I hate you!" Angela shrieked at the top of her voice. "I'm so mad at you I could kill you! I hate you! I hate you!"

Everyone in the hall stopped. Bennett stood, frozen in absolute shock.

Instead of going to first period, Bennett decided he'd go to see Mr. Whitby. When he got there, Mr. Whitby was in the back cleaning out his closet.

"Hi, Mr. Whitby," Bennett said ever so humbly.

"Don't speak to me, blabber mouth. I have nothing to say to you. And if I did, it wouldn't be anything you'd like to hear."

"But, Mr. Whitby..."

"But? But what! You've just ended all my hopes of becoming a professor. Something I worked my tail off for."

"But I..."

"Forget it! Now get outta my sight and fast!" Bennett left the classroom with mixed feelings. He was angry and yet sorry for Mr. Whitby.

"Listen up, you guys! Listen up!" Coach Dee ordered while in the meeting room. "Okay, guys," the coach spoke in almost a whisper, "here's the plan against New Rochelle." All of a sudden there was a knock on the door. Dexter answered it. It was the little red-haired freshman who loved the team.

"Yeah, Redd, what do you want?" Dexter said.

"Bennett, someone is here to see you!" the little guy shouted into the room.

"Tell the person, Bennett will be there in a few minutes, I'm going over some material," Coach Dee said on Bennett's behalf. Like the rest of the team, Coach thought it was a hungry reporter craving for Bennett's interview. Bennett was hounded by the newspapers more than ever since he signed that letter of intent to Columbia, a few weeks ago.

Coach Dee designed his plays on the chalkboard and the team huddled in a circle and shouted, "Knights!" They then ran out in ascending order, from the shortest to the tallest.

On the way to the gym, Bennett broke formation when he spotted Redd.

"Who wants me?"

"It's a man wearin' a funny-lookin' hat and a patch over his eye. He gave me ten bucks—look!"

"Yeah, I see. Now, where is he?"

"He's down over there. He said that's where he would be." Redd pointed downstairs to the left. So that's where Bennett went.

Two men stood in the downstairs bathroom. "Blood...Willie and I were beginnin' to think you wasn't gonna show." Simon blew cigar smoke into the air. "Shh," Willie whispered, as a toilet flushed. No one appeared. "Who's in there!" Willie said. Willie, a big bald-headed dude, had a scarred-up face and a deep, vibrating voice. Definitely not the type of guy you'd want to see on a dark street.

A little voice answered. "It's me, Redd."

Bennett was surprised. "Redd, how did you get in here?"

"I came through the other door."

"Okay. Now go out that door."

"Is it all clear now?" Simon said.

"Yeah, all clear." Bennett responded after checking.

"Say, Blood, you look a little uptight. Some of this, here...will loosen you right up."

"Yo, Simon. You know, I don't do no weed! Put that junk away."

"All right, Blood, all right, here ya go." Simon handed him a roll of dollar bills—one hundred—to try and brighten his mood.

"I didn't earn that."

"I know you didn't. At least not yet."

"What do you mean, *not yet*? Look man, I told you before ..."

"I know what you told me before. Obviously...I'll tell you what. We won't discuss it any further, but if Mt. Vernon should happen to lose, this is yours," Simon said and held the roll of bills next to Bennett's face.

The game had already started when Bennett got up to the gym. Hezekiah started in his place, but when he got in the game, it was all Bennett. Bennett from the left side. Bennett from the right side. Bennett from the top of the key. He was ubiquitous.

Bennett was doing it all until the second half when he started playing like a drunken old man. Nobody knew what was wrong with him. The team felt he was due for at least forty-five points. He had twenty-five in the first half alone.

With just two seconds left and down by one, Bennett threw up an off-balance hook that popped off the rim. The good Lord was with them. Bennett drew a foul. By scoring only four points in the second half, he was at twenty-nine for the game. If he sank the two free throws, Mt. Vernon would win the game. The game was in Bennett's hands.

The gym grew silent while Bennett procrastinated with the ball. Once it found its final destination, it flirted with the rim and sluggishly rolled in. The crowd cheered because the game was tied. By this time Kirby saw Simon get up and make his way down the bleacher seats on the opposite side of the gym, his loyal acolyte following. Bennett stepped away from the line to catch his breath and regain his equilibrium. He went back to the line, bounced the ball several times, hesitated, bounced again, bent his knees, walked away and then returned to the line. He released the ball high and soft, with a back spin you wouldn't believe. And like slow motion, the ball swished through the hoop.

The gymnasium exploded with 'Bennett-Mania.' The crowd erupted; some ran onto the floor while others celebrated from the stands, chanting, "BEN-nett! BEN-nett! BEN-nett!"

The team had to fight its way back to the locker room.

Once they were in, Kirby made his way toward Bennett.

"Ay, man, who was that person who wanted to see you before the game that had you out of the starting lineup? Was it a sportswriter?"

"No," Bennett said closing his locker.

"Who was it then, a scout?" Kirby said, even though he already had an inkling.

"It was that cat who wanted to see me last week with all that cash."

"You didn't take any, did you!"

"Calm down...I didn't take anything."

"You sure?" Kirby said. "Because your scholarship is down the drain if you're caught. You could also get in trouble with the law."

"Please, I know all that," Bennett raised both hands, "Don't you trust me?"

"You know me better than that. It's him I don't trust. Bennett, stay away from that turkey. He's bad news. Real bad. He's also dangerous. Look what happened to Stinky."

"Leave Stinky out of this. Did you tell anybody?"

"No. I didn't tell nobody. But be careful. Don't be fooled by him. People look up to you. You can't get involved with him, you just can't."

"Look," Bennett said reassuringly, "he knows what's up. You see I didn't throw the game, right?"

"What! He asked you again to throw the game?"

"Shh, Kirby, calm down. First of all, I don't have to answer to nobody but Betty Wilson."

"Yeah, right," Kirby answered bitterly. "Bennett, stay away from that guy. He's no good! Look, I still have the scars from you almost beatin' me to death because I was hangin' out with those dope pushers."

"Yeah, so what are you sayin'?"

"Again...after what just happened to Stinky, and you tellin' me, I would only be a loser to get involved with that mess."

"Kirby, I told you before I wasn't gonna do no dealin' with him. I don't even know his real name. He gave me some jive-time name, Simon...Simon Diamond."

"What kind of name is that?"

"Man, I don't know."

"Well, I'll see you later." Now I know why he was playing so funny in the second half, Kirby thought to himself.

"Yeah, later." Bennett said and left. It wasn't too long after he was gone when Kirby realized Bennett had forgotten his books. No problem he thought, he'd run them by his job this evening.

❦

"Hi, my name is Kirby. Are you Bennett's boss?"

"I'm Bill, what can I do for you?"

"Is Bennett around? I'd like to talk with him."

"No, I'm afraid he isn't," Bill said, wiping his hands dry with a towel.

"No?" Kirby said. "Where is he, home? Was he sick?"

"He's not sick. But he may be home, though."

"What do you mean?"

"Bennett was fired."

"Fired?" Kirby shouted. "For what!"

"For sleeping." Bill turned his back, moved away a few feet, then returned. "I told him time after time, if he wanted to sleep on the job, he should find himself a night watchman's job, or somethin'. I warned him several times. I just couldn't take it anymore. But he's a good kid, I wish him well."

"Yeah, okay," Kirby sighed. "Well, did he say where he was goin', whether it would be home or not?"

"No, as a matter of fact, he didn't."

"Thanks, Bill, take care. I'll see you around."

Kirby walked down the cold, dark streets and had flashes of Bennett receiving patsy money from Simon. Every time he saw the image in his mind, the pores of his skin would open. When he was a half-block away, he spotted Simon's dark blue Cadillac parked in front of Bennett's building.

Willie got out of the driver's side and then Bennett and Simon emerged from the back. Kirby lost his cool and started running toward them.

"Bennett! Bennett! Bennett!" he shouted. "What are you doin' with this guy?"

"Guy!" Simon said. "I'm a man. That's *sir* to you...chump."

"Shut up, bama. I'm about two seconds off you, anyway."

"Watch yourself, kid!" Big Willie said.

"Aw, Moose, you ain't scarin' nobody."

"Some other time, Willie. Some other time," Simon said and went for his car.

"Yo, man, it's cool," Bennett said to Simon as he and Willie drove off.

"Bennett, I'm surprised at you. What's wrong with you?"

"I'm surprised at you!"

"For what!"

"For thinkin' of me like that. That's what!" Bennett started walking slowly toward the building.

"So, why were you with him, then?"

"What are you, Kirby, a sissy or somethin'?" Bennett said angrily. "For your information, Mr. Maxwell," Bennett stopped walking, "I was just fired."

"So, what took you so long, to get home, then?" Kirby said equally annoyed. "I know what happened. Here's your books."

"Look," Bennett said and snatched his books, "when he saw me walkin', he pulled over and I got in. He saw I was upset, so he treated me to pizza. That's all! No money involved," Bennett said brushing Kirby aside. "Now if you'll excuse me, I gotta go tell Momma."

"She's not home now, is she?"

"Well, when she gets home then. And Kirby," Bennett said with his back facing him, "bug off!"

Kirby began to get real scared for Bennett. He wasn't sure Bennett even remembered his own name anymore. He just didn't seem the same. Kirby was sure Bennett hadn't taken any money. But, he also felt, it was just a matter of time. Especially with him now out of work and not looking terribly depressed.

"Hey, Yvette," Bennett said entering the apartment. "Champ, still up?"

"Yeah, he's in the tub. Why you home so early?"

"The tub?" Bennett said overlooking Yvette's question.

"I told him not to go in."

"Hey, Champ," Bennett opened the bathroom door, "come on man, get outta that tub. Do you know what time it is? You have school in the mornin'!"

"Okay, Bennett."

"What's wrong, Yvette?" Bennett said as he walked back into the kitchen. "You look sad, Pumpkin. Tell me what's wrong. Champ gettin' on your nerves?"

"Here, Bennett," Yvette said handing him a letter.

"What's this?"

"Momma got a dispossess," Yvette said.

"And I lost my job today. Oh, man...we have to have payment, in full within seven days. If not, we have to leave in the next thirty days. Does Momma know yet?" Bennett staggered to the sofa.

"No, Bennett, are you all right?"

"Yeah, I'm okay."

"But, you almost fell."

"I'm all right."

"Hi, Big Bra!" Dannon raced from the bathroom wearing his Spiderman pajamas.

"Oh, hi Champ," Bennett answered weakly.

"Could I have a ride?"

"No, just come sit down."

"What's wrong?" Dannon said and sat next to his big brother. "Are you, gonna, die? Because I don't want you to. Big Bra, I love you."

"What makes you say that! Tell me why you say that?" Bennett said again, only this time a little more frightened.

"It was one mornin', when I woke up to go to the kitchen. I heard you yellin', real loud, 'I don't want to die. No, No, No!' I got scared, Big Bra." He laid his head in Bennett's lap and started sobbing.

Bennett kept his eyes on his younger sibling and thought how much he really loved him. "No," Bennett said, "I'm not dyin'."

"For a long time, you promise?"

"Don't worry," Bennett said, wiping away Dannon's tears.

"You go to bed now, okay? I'll be there in a little while to tuck you in. Now go on," Bennett patted Dannon on the rear.

"Same goes for you, Pumpkin."

"I want to wait up for Momma."

"No, you go to bed. I'll wait up."

"Okay, good night."

"Good night."

"Hi Momma," Bennett said, languid-eyed on the sofa. He tried desperately to stay awake for her.

"Hi, Baby. You just gettin' home?"

"No, Momma," Bennett said sorrowfully. "I've been here..I was fired today." He reached out to embrace her.

"Aw, son, that's quite all right," Mrs. Wilson said with affection as she patted him on the back.

"But Momma, we got a dispossess."

"Where is it?" He went over to the kitchen table, picked up the letter and handed it to her.

"We'll be fine. You'll see, baby. We'll be fine. You go on to bed, and I'll see you in the mornin'." Without another word, he went back to the sofa.

CHAPTER TWELVE

The following day he didn't go to school nor did he attend practice. In fact, Kirby didn't see him until 11:30 that night, when he came to Kirby's house, "Kirby, I was out all day, job huntin', that's where I was."

"Did you find anything?"

"No. I did not," he answered, punching his right fist into his left palm.

"Go home and sleep on it, Bennett... things will eventually get better."

"Maybe, you're right, I'll see you later."

"Okay, you guys. You all see what's going on out there! You're embarrassing yourselves! We're down by twenty points! You guys aren't even trying! You, Bennett. You're the center of attention. You have scouts out there looking at you. I don't mean just college scouts either. There are about five or six professional scouts out there, and you're playing like you have lead in your shorts."

Bennett remained quiet during Coach Dee's tirade. Kirby wasn't surprised that Bennett was tongueless, but he was dumbfounded that

Bennett was letting problems affect his play, knowing Bennett, and how much he loved basketball.

"And you, Dex," Coach continued his harangue, "one of our best defensive players. You're playing, matador defense and you let Roke Smith light you up for thirty points."

"It's twenty-nine points!" Dexter corrected.

"That's just as bad, and shut up while I'm talking! You know better." The room grew so quiet at Coach Dee's fury you could hear the blood running through your veins.

"Now look, fellas. You better watch and study these diagrams carefully if you want to get back in this thing. Now look, and listen."

The team huddled and yelled, "Knights!" Everyone, that is, except Bennett.

In the second half, Bennett scored twenty points in the first five minutes and the game was hot like fire. Nip and tuck and full of excitement, even though both teams already earned spots in the playoffs. The intensity level hit new highs in the final twenty seconds. The score was 95-94 Gorton.

Roke Smith, a slender guy about Bennett's height, who could jump out of the building if he wanted, was dribbling up court against Dexter. Dexter, who had been taken advantage of, by Roke, to the tune of forty points, was determined not to let him score again to win the game.

Roke faked left and went right, causing Dexter to slip to the floor. Dexter regained his position and continued to dog with defense. When the clock ticked down to five seconds, Roke dribbled over to the right baseline to take a twenty-foot jumpshot. Dexter was still dogging. As Roke reached his spot, he posted quickly to take flight. But as he leaped into the air, Dexter, who remained planted, waited until Roke hit his apex and yanked him by the shorts. The shorts fell past his knees, exposing jock strap, cup and all. The crowd roared.

When Roke finally landed, he floored Dexter, with a right hook to the jaw. Bennett ran toward Roke, who still had his shorts down to his ankles. When Bennett reached him, Shorty Stokes, the Gorton point-guard, ran over and sucker-punched him in the back of the head. Reeling from the unexpected hit, Bennett turned and socked Shorty in the mouth, knocking out his two front teeth and splattering blood all over the place.

Hence, pandemonium broke loose. The benches and bleachers cleared; players and fans from both sides charged onto the court. The gym was a massive sight of fists, book bags and pocketbooks. The horror show lasted five minutes, before the police arrived and finally re-established control.

The next day the police reported over twenty-five arrested and over a hundred injuries. Twenty of the injuries were serious.

The arrest and injury count wasn't as relative as the news Bennett received later that evening.

"Turn the music down, Kirby!" Bennett yelled. "I got Coach on the phone."

"Bennett," Coach Dee spoke softly. "I am really very sorry. Columbia has rescinded your scholarship due to what they consider a violation of the moral clause in your contract. Headlines like MT. VERNON STAR IGNITES GYMNASIUM BRAWL didn't help."

"They wouldn't consider givin' me another chance, Coach?"

"I'm afraid not, Bennett. I tried. I tried real hard."

"I know you did, Coach."

"Bennett, they're other schools...hundreds of them, that..."

"I know, Coach," Bennett said, as he began to tremble with anger.

"Well, if you need anything, you know where to find me."

Kirby saw the anguish in Bennett's face as he spoke. Bennett covered his eyes with his fists and shrieked, "I lost everything!"

"Lost what, Bennett?" Dannon asked.

"Go in the room with Yvette," Kirby told Dannon, pushing him off gently.

"Kirby, I lost my girl! My job! My scholarship! We're about to get kicked out of this apartment! What more?" Bennett took off for the door with such speed that he almost knocked over his mother, who was returning from grocery shopping.

"What's wrong?" she said fearfully.

"Bennett! Bennett! Bennett!" Kirby shouted down the stairway. But to no avail. He went back inside to tell Mrs. Wilson what had happened. Before he could finish, she broke into tears. After she heard the whole story, her tears continued to roll. She wept, thinking how hard Bennett worked to accomplish something positive in life, and now he had lost what he wanted most. Kirby tried to comfort her, but he didn't feel he was successful.

Bennett walked through the dark streets of Mt. Vernon oblivious to what was going on around him. He wasn't aware that he passed several people shooting dope and two young boys running away after snatching a pocketbook from an elderly lady, and that he narrowly escaped becoming a quadriplegic by being hit by a car...twice. He was so far out of it that it was frightening.

He wandered around for several hours before he approached an alley. With his massive hands, he grabbed the top off a garbage can, and pounded it against the wall. "Why? Why? Why? Why? Why?" He shouted and shouted until he was overcome with exhaustion. The pressure being too much for him, he collapsed.

Hours later, he woke up, the sun shining brightly in his eyes. Squinting to neutralize the sun, he saw he was sitting between two derelicts who looked to have claimed that spot even before he was an itch in his daddy's pants. He scrambled to his feet and ran out of the alley.

"Son, where were you?" His mother's voice trembled as she embraced him. "I was worried sick. Where have you been, son?"

"Momma," Bennett said sadly, "I passed out in an alley. Momma, I don't know what's wrong with me. Before things were goin' along so good...so great. Then all of a sudden, disaster hit." Bennett walked over to his sofa bed. "I'm scared for myself."

"Oh, son, don't be scared," Mrs. Wilson said, placing her hand on his knee as she sat next to him. "Don't worry baby, you'll overcome. Just have a lil' faith."

"But..."

"Sometimes son, the good Lord in all His infinite wisdom will test you with the things you love most, just to see how strong you are and how long you can endure."

"Momma," his mother's comforting words seemed to do wonders as he said, "you mean like Job in the Bible?"

"Exactly, son." Mrs. Wilson kissed him on the forehead. "Now, you go on and get cleaned up and I'll fix you some breakfast. And remember...Momma loves you very much and she's very proud of you."

"Okay, Momma. Thanks."

"Oh, I better call Kirby. He's been worried sick," Mrs. Wilson said.

"Okay," Bennett said again and stripped off his jacket and headed for the bathroom.

"Hello."

"Hello, Kirby."

"Mrs. Wilson!" Kirby choked as he sat up in bed.

"Yes."

"Is Bennett all right?"

"Yes, don't worry. He's home now."

"Thank God," Kirby breathed with relief. "May I speak to him?"

"He's in the shower now," she said. "But I have an idea. Since your Momma ain't home, you get dressed, come upstairs and have breakfast with Bennett. He really needs you now."

"Be right up."

"Don't forget to wash your face first," Mrs. Wilson teased.

Not long after the telephone conversation, he was upstairs.

"Yo, Bennett, what's up for today?" Kirby called out from the kitchen.

"What's up, Kirb," returned a voice from the bathroom. "I don't know. I think I'll play some ball."

"Play ball? Man it's fifty degrees outside," Kirby responded.

Bennett countered, "Fifty degrees, so what? With body heat and sweat, you have twenty more degrees. Then it'll be seventy, see?"

"Mrs. Wilson, you have one crazy son."

"Don't I know it, Kirby! Don't I know it!"

"With all the excitement going on, I forgot to tell you."

"Tell me what?"

"Jimmy Jones called me last night. He said there's a spot for me—a starting spot with the Sonics at the Boys' Club, when our season is over."

"Oh," Bennett said. "Somebody's grandfather backed out and can't play?"

"Very funny, but I'll have you know that I'm joining an elite group."

"What are you talking about?"

"The Mount Vernon Boy's South Side Club is home to some of the finest ball players in New York."

"Like I wouldn't know that. I'm a member; I'm one of them. That reminds me. I have to get in touch with Billy Thomas. He wants to know if I can help him out with his basketball camp this summer."

"Are you gonna do it?"

"Of course, I'll look out. Besides, I can get Dannon in there for free being one of the instructors and Billy Tee is my man."

"Yeah," Kirby agreed. "He's good people. So what are you trying to do, pass the torch?"

"Hey, Dannon can shoot. He has a good eye for the basket."

"But isn't what you're gonna do called *nepotism?*"

Bennett started to laugh but then answered, "Yeah...so what."

The conversation was briefly discontinued as the two young men gulped down the delicious breakfast of sausage, eggs, toast, hash browns, fried apples and freshly squeezed orange juice with shaved ice. That is until Bennett had a notion and offered, "The

Boys' Club is a positive place for kids. I hope that it'll add somethin' positive to your declinin' game."

"Aw, Ben-Ben," Kirby lamented through a playful act of sadness. "I thought you were my man—my main man."

"You know I am, Kirby. But, let's face it, your game is like the economy."

"What do you mean?"

"Your game is in recession. Anyway, whose spot are you takin'?"

"Lowes Moore's. He's supposed to have a tryout with a semi-pro team up in Canada."

Bennett nodded his head in approval after he took a few sips of orange juice.

"He's got a good jumpshot, a great handle and he can pass out of this world. He should make it. He probably would have to get a little stronger though."

"I hope he does too. I want to keep my spot."

"Let's roll, Kirb," Bennett said, putting on his jacket. "What's for lunch?"

"Lunch? What do you mean? We just had breakfast. Am I supposed to be treatin'?"

"Yeah, sure...Cromwell's?"

Kirby almost gagged. "Cromwell's? Are you out of your mind? I owe you two burgers at Fancy's and that's as far as it goes."

"Kirby," Bennett said with a smile, "you drive a hard bargain."

"Got to." Kirby went over to press for the elevator.

"Besides, I haven't seen Charley in a long time."

Bennett seemed withdrawn on the way to the park. Finally, Kirby said, "Bennett, you okay man?"

"I don't know," he said. "That's why I didn't want to stay in the house."

"Bennett, if you ever need somebody to talk to, you know where I am."

"I know it." The two slapped five.

"I'll say this..."

"We're here," Bennett said, stepping into the park.

Kirby held him back. "So what. Bennett, I want to tell you somethin'."

"What, man?"

"Listen, Bennett, you've helped me overcome a lot of stuff. Some stuff you never even knew about. So I'm sayin' to you...stay away from that bama, Simon what's-his-name. He's nothin' but trouble for..."

"Kirby, haven't we had this dance before? Besides, what do I have to lose? I've lost everything, and we may be homeless soon. What else is there?"

"Bennett," Kirby said, "what else is there? I guess, you don't realize how much respect you have around here. Ay, it ain't many that would even attempt to do what you did: go to school full-time; work a part-time job, with weird, crazy hours; play an organized sport—that's your meal ticket to a quality, free education; deal with your mother's illness; and be a father figure to Dannon and Yvette. You're a righteous, black man. You should be proud of yourself!"

"Ay, man, let's shoot." Bennett pulled away.

❧◉☙

"Ay, Charley....What's up? Long time no see."

"I'm hip. Kirby tells me you've been workin' lately."

"Lately is right," Bennett said.

"What do you mean? You been laid off or somethin?"

"Yeah, I was caught in dreamland a few times."

"I can dig it," Charley said. "Well, what will you two have? It's on the house."

"Really?"

"Just this time because Bennett here hasn't been around in such a long while."

"Okay then, Charley, we'll have the usual," Kirby said.

"Two usuals it is." Charley walked away from the booth. When Charley was gone, Kirby said, "I hear some talk of Shorty gettin' some guys after you."

Bennett looked up from the menu. "How do you know?"

"Kathy called me this mornin'. She heard Shorty spent all night in the hospital. You didn't just knock out his two front teeth, you also did some serious damage to his gums."

"Shorty ain't nothin' but a lil' punk. Not only that, he shouldn't have snuck me. I was only tryin' to break everything up."

"I know."

"Besides," Bennett said, "I'm not afraid of anyone anyway, so let's just forget about it."

"Forgotten."

"Ay, Charley!" Bennett said. "Where's our grub!"

"Comin' right up," Charley nodded and brought over the cheeseburgers, fries and shakes.

"Ay, Bennett, I just heard you lost your scholarship to Columbia."

"Who told you that?" Bennett asked.

"Franky just told me," Charley motioned toward the kitchen.

"Franky?"

"Bennett, don't you remember? Him and Coach Dee played baseball together in high school. They still hang out together."

"Franky? Oh yeah, Franky, the Frank Square. The man, who made the phrase, 'L-seven', popular." Franky was the cook with the chrome dome shaped like a box.

"Well, is it true?"

"Yeah, Charley, it's true."

"So, what's next? I wish I had an openin' here." Charley placed the food on the table.

"Thanks anyway, Charley, but I'll just play it by ear. Somethin' will come up, I'm sure...I hope."

"You seem to be takin' it pretty well."

"Charley, this is a front. I hurt all inside."

"I hear you. Well, I gotta take care of my other customers before I lose them. Take care, Bennett. Don't be a stranger."

The two life-long friends gulped down the food like there was no tomorrow.

"That was pretty good."

"Yeah, I can tell," Kirby said with a smile, looking at his companion's empty plate.

"Man, I don't know what to do now, but I certainly don't feel like goin' home yet. It's only three o'clock."

They decided to stay and talk about future plans. Although Bennett was suffering, he tried to keep sunny thoughts. They conversed about family, college, working, basketball, his troubles. They even spoke about Tara.

Before they knew it, an hour and a half had gone by. Suddenly, four mysterious looking compeers entered. Kirby felt knots growing in his stomach.

The foursome stood at the entrance and looked around. Every single one of them seemed serious. Two had on very dark shades. One was sporting a clean-bean haircut and the other a big bushy— but neat—Afro. They sat in the booth across from them. Thinking about it, Kirby knew they were trouble. He began to get jittery while Bennett, who kept talking, stayed cool, calm and collected. "Yo, Bennett, do you want to leave?"

"No." Bennett looked over at the other booth. "For what?"

"I don't know. I thought you might want to leave, that's all."

"Naw, we can stay a lil' while longer." He glanced at the Mickey Mouse clock on the wall. "It's only four-thirty."

Bennett and Kirby continued their conversation when suddenly a French fry landed in their booth. It just missed Bennett's nose. He ignored it and kept speaking. "Ay, Bennett, man," Kirby stood up, "I wanna get outta here, and quick fast."

"Just sit back down and be cool. That's all. Be cool." Kirby sat down, then suddenly the guy with the bushy 'fro grabbed a handful of fries. Just as Kirby said to himself, Oh no, the guy stood up and threw them, hitting Bennett on his neck and Kirby in the face. They were smudged with ketchup and grease.

Bennett got up with fire in his eyes and his partner followed. Kirby was ready to throw down, as all of his nervousness exploded into anger. Bennett charged the other booth. As the clean-bean attempted to get up, Bennett obliged. He palmed clean-bean's collar in his right hand to bring him to his feet and caved in his gut with the left. One of the other guys with shades broke from the booth and charged at Bennett who was in a fighting stance. Kirby intercepted the charging hood with a leaping elbow to the jaw. It sent them both to the floor. Kirby got up. The hood didn't.

"Stop it, before I call the police!" Charley screamed from behind the counter.

"Bennett! Watch out!" Kirby shouted. The other shaded creep was about to sneak Bennett. With a swift turn of the head, Bennett capped him in the jaw. Before he could turn back around, the dude with the bushy 'fro was on Bennett's blind side. This one was Kirby's. His kick to the ribs was devastating. The bully's fall was temporarily interrupted by a broken lopsided chair, but Kirby kicked and kicked until his overmatched foe lay unconscious.

"You guys better get outta here before they come to," Charley warned. Bennett and Kirby looked at each other, smiled, exchanged fives and took off.

When they reached their building, they slapped five again. "See ya tomorrow mornin', Batman."

"You got it, Robin," Kirby came back as Bennett ran up the stairs.

"W-W-What's up? M-M-Man, w-what ha-happened t-t-to..."

"My face?" Kirby said, nodding his head.

"Y-Y-Yeah," Big Joe said to Kirby as they stood amidst the crowded hallway, after third period class.

"Bennett and I got into a fight..."

"W-W-With each other?"

"No, man. Shorty got some guys after Bennett, and we had to take care of them...bar room brawl style."

"Wh-Wh-Where's B-B-Bennett?" Joe said, feeling a bit deprived because he missed the big rumble.

"He's in Coach Dee's office."

❧

"Hey, Bennett," Coach Dee greeted.

"Ay Coach, what's up?" Bennett closed the glass door behind him.

"First of all, Bennett, I'd like you to meet Mr. William Steinburg of KWN-TV." The two shook hands. Mr. Steinburg was a salt and pepper-haired man with a pot belly.

"I won't beat around the bush, Mr. Wilson," Steinburg said. "Although your scholarship has been withdrawn, KWN-TV would like to have you, along with another athlete on your team, as a special guest on our Saturday morning sports show, 'Tomorrow's Pros.' We will donate $2,000 to the school's scholarship fund. One thousand each, in the names of Bennett Wilson and the other athlete. Your coach here has recommended Joe Hancock."

Bennett was looking at him, somewhat befuddled. "Who? Me and Big Joe on TV?"

"Yes, that's correct. So, do we have a deal? Will you come on our show?"

"Sure, I will. But I'm not so sure Joe will. Joe don't talk to the press. He stutters."

"Well, we'll have to see that he accepts, won't we?" Coach Dee said.

Excitedly, Bennett said, "Yeah, I guess we'll have to, won't we?"

"So it's a deal," Steinburg said. "Saturday morning at seven we'll have a limousine waiting downstairs for you. Breakfast is on us. Same goes for Joe. And, he shouldn't worry because since you're the star and captain of the team, you'll do most of the talking."

"Okay. Anyway, he'll like the eatin' part." Bennett stood, proud and elated. "But, Joe and I don't live in the same buildin'."

"That's taken care of already," Steinburg said. His next sentence was interrupted by the school bell. "Well, I'd better be gettin' off to class now," Bennett said.

"Don't forget to tell Joe, Bennett!" Coach Dee shouted. Just then, Bennett was out the door.

The week went by, Bennett and Big Joe appeared on TV along with two other players from Hempstead High, Damon Jacobs and Fitzgerald Grey.

Bennett's family and neighbors celebrated his being on TV as did Joe's. Bennett's popularity, which was never really hidden under a microscope, was even more considerable now.

One day after school, Bennett went to Hartley Park, located in the bourgeois section of Mt. Vernon near Tara's house.

Hartley Park was famous for its serene atmosphere, a place for lovers, elderly people, or those who just want to get away.

Bennett must've spent at least two hours thinking while sitting on a beautifully carved wooden park bench, when he heard a familiar, "Say, Youngblood, what's happenin'?"

"Ay, man, what are you doin' here?" Bennett asked as Simon sat next to him.

"I come to this park all the time. I'm a nature freak. Question is, what are you doin' here? I saw you on TV the other day. You looked real good. But, your partner...what's his name...Joe Hancock?"

"Yeah."

"He made me laugh so hard when he broke that chair, I almost wet myself."

You probably did, Bennett thought to himself. "That was funny," Bennett offered. "They had to interrupt the show just so they could calm him down. And thanks for sayin' I looked good, but I have somethin' to figure out."

"Oh, like a job, scholarship, your old lady?"

"Hey, how did you know about my girl?"

"I know a lot about you, Youngblood."

"Say what?"

"Like you bein' put out of your apartment." Simon smiled. He was proud of himself.

"Who told you that?" Bennett jumped to his feet. "Who told you that?"

Simon persisted, "What about your mother havin' high blood pressure and barely able to work?"

"Yo, man, you've been spyin' on me. I don't like people spyin' on me!" Bennett stormed away. Simon was on his heels.

"Say, Youngblood, if you will just listen a minute, I have a proposition, I'm sure you won't refuse."

"Stuff it!"

"Oh well," he said, "if you want your Momma, sister and little brother to be put out on the streets, then...keep goin'."

"I have an aunt. She lives a few blocks away."

"Who, Daisy?" Simon said. "Daisy stays so blasted, she doesn't know where she lives, let alone take you all in."

"How do you know about Daisy?" Bennett felt outclassed and started walking slowly toward Simon. "You give her junk, too? You creep!"

"Calm down, Blood." Simon smiled again. "I always stay close to my clients."

"I'm not your client," Bennett shot back. "I'm nobody's client. I don't work."

"I know that. Bill let you go for sleepin'. I know...that's why I'm here. Just lookin' out for a brother. Come back in the park." Simon flashed a roll of one hundred dollar bills that put Bennett in a trance.

"Say, Blood," Simon said, his arm laid across the back of the bench. "Remember the New Ro' game? I asked you to throw it. But..."

"But what?"

"Listen first, Youngblood. That's over and done with. I'm willin' to make amends. Not only that, I wanted to see if you were an easy safe to crack."

"Well, you saw I ain't." Bennett got up from the park bench. He felt the momentum skidding back in his direction.

"I know that." Simon rose, placing his hand on Bennett's shoulder. "I know that. That's why I'm...well, me and my establishment are bettin' for Mt. Vernon to win the championship. You see, Youngblood, I'm not askin' you to throw a game anymore. I'm just gonna ask you not to win by more than five points. That means you can't have another forty-point outburst."

"Let me get this straight," Bennett said. "You mean you're not askin' me to throw the game, but you're askin' me not to score forty points and not to win by more than five points. Is that it?"

"Yeah, Blood, that's it! You see, man, right now you don't have that scholarship and you don't have a job. Before, I could understand—you had all that to lose. Now, you don't. They're gone already!"

"My man, there are plenty of other scholarship offers."

"I know. I also know you don't want those other scholarships. You wanted to make your mark at that big Ivy League school in New York City." Simon's crack quickly wiped the smile off Bennett's face.

"Can you drive?" Again, Simon was gaining the advantage.

"Yeah, I..."

"Solid! I'll supply you with all the transportation you need. Youngblood, about college, you will have enough money to pay for your college, your sister's college, and your brother's college. And, about the honeys! You can take 'em anywhere and buy 'em anything. You'll have so much bread, you'll be able to look that green-eyed guy from the honor society right in the eye. You'll be on his level. This will definitely help your mother's situation. Not only with the rent. Shoot! What you're gonna get, you can make a down payment on a house. As for her high blood pressure, the relief of being in a new, fresh house, will do wonders, as far as her recovery is concerned...Then, you'll really be on rich boy's level...A house!" Bennett's head was spinning, like a top. "I'll tell you what, Blood."

"What?"

"Today's Wednesday, the championship game isn't until Sunday. Up in Glen Falls, right?"

"Right."

"Well, you take awhile to think about it. I'll see you sometime on Friday just before you board the bus. By the way," Simon said, "what time does it leave?"

"Five-thirty, in front of City Hall."

"Be there. Later on, Blood."

Simon left and Bennett was not himself. Simon had clearly won this round.

CHAPTER THIRTEEN

"What's up Bennett?" Bennett greeted Kirby at the door and let him in. "Where did you go today? You missed a good practice." Bennett sat down on the couch.

"To Hartley Park."

"With who?" Kirby asked. "Shana, Jamie, Becky?"

"Becky?"

"Yeah Becky, what's wrong with her?"

"What's wrong? Man, that girl's breath stinks...Knocks the life out of you."

"Say, Bennett, what's that word again?...hali...?"

"Halitosis?

"Yeah! That's it...halitosis! Sorry I asked," Kirby said returning Bennett's smile. "Then who?" Kirby reverted to the previous subject.

"What's with the third degree, Kirby? For your information, I was by myself, that is, until Simon came along."

"Simon! I thought you got rid of him! Bennett, don't tell me..."

"Right now, I haven't anything to lose. There's nothin' left."

"Now, Bennett," Kirby sat in the rocking chair across from him. "Push comes to shove you know if you need somewhere to stay, you can stay at my house. You know that."

"I know."

"About your scholarship. I know you say you're not interested, but plenty of other schools would love to have you. Don't tell me you've stopped gettin' letters, because you haven't. Man, you were even on TV. Of course other schools would love to have you."

"How do you know?" Bennett sucked in some air.

"Because, I know. That's how. About a job, you know somethin' will eventually come up. Maybe the same one, once Bill cools off. And as for Tara, you know good and well, she still loves you very much. She hasn't even looked at another guy since the breakup."

"Yeah? How about Sol? They're always together...Mr. Green Eyes."

"Well, if you didn't only half speak to her, she would've told you by now."

"Told me what?"

"Number one," Kirby said, "Sol Weiss is real tight with this girl named Ashley, who goes to New Ro'. I even heard they're gonna go to the same college and maybe get married after the first year there. Number two, if you'd speak to her, she would've told you why she was with him so much. It wasn't just for studyin'. She was tryin' to get you accepted into the Honor Society."

"What!"

"That's right," Kirby said. "See, by the time you and her started actually goin' together, it was far too late for anyone to get accepted. But with her bein' vice president and Sol bein' president, she figured they could work somethin' out. She loves you, man, so much that she was riskin' her neck to get you in. It was all to help increase your standin' at Columbia. Everybody knows how prestigious that school is."

"Yeah, right."

"You are so pig-headed man!"

Bennett stood up, walked toward Kirby and pointed, "Forget Tara! Forget Sol! Forget Columbia! And the Honor Society! I don't need them!"

"Bennett..."

"And forget you, too!"

"Now, I know you don't mean that."

"Oh, yeah?" Bennett said. "What makes you so sure I don't? Have you ever known me to lie?"

Kirby wavered. He waited for a response. Bennett was serious. "Okay, man. Have it your way." Kirby left the apartment.

Kirby was grieved by the encounter. Not so much by what was said to him personally, but what was said about things Bennett loved so much. Kirby hadn't told Coach Dee—or anyone for that matter—about Bennett's meetings with a hustler. Big Joe knew about Simon, but not about Simon and Bennett. Kirby felt it was his responsibility to deter Bennett from doing something that would jeopardize his future and his life.

For the rest of that week, Bennett came to school only for practice. During practice, he didn't say one word to Kirby. A couple of times, he looked Kirby's way, but that was all. Everyone on the team stuck close to Bennett. It was obvious to them that he was going through some rough times. Kirby knew why. He prayed and spent sleepless nights worrying about his buddy.

Finally, Mt. Vernon was headed to the big game. Maybe Bennett and Kirby would get it together then.

"All aboard!" the bus driver announced sounding like a train conductor.

"Say, Coach, we gotta get on this yellow piece of junk?" Kirby asked before boarding.

It was a question Kirby already knew the answer to.

"I'll tell you what, Kirby," Coach Dee said. "It's about a five-hour drive. But, if you start walkin' now, it should take you no longer than a month to get there."

Coach noticed Bennett standing several feet away. "Who's that Bennett's talkin' to over there? Hey, Bennett, come on!" Coach yelled. Kirby got on the bus hastily. Coach wasn't going to hear anything from him.

"Comin' Coach!"

"Well, Blood, if you didn't decide yet, I guess I could wait until we get up there. So you have a safe trip. Later." Simon and Bennett slapped five.

"One more thing, Blood," Simon said just before walking away. "I know how you feel about it, but try some of this stuff here. It'll really loosen you up, relax you, make you feel good all over." Bennett didn't explode with anger, like times past, when Simon offered him drugs. "Take it." Simon tucked it in Bennett's bag. "They're already rolled up for you. Smoke some, before you go to bed tonight and in the mornin' when you first get up. Believe me, you'll feel like a new man. You'll forget all your troubles."

"I can certainly use somethin' to help me forget about all this stuff goin' on."

"I hear ya," Simon said and walked away. "Oh, by the way," Simon made his way back toward Bennett, "don't smoke any just before game time…first thing in the mornin' is usually best."

"Okay," Bennett said and darted off for the bus as Coach Dee yelled for him again.

Kirby sat in the middle of the bus with Big Joe. Bennett sat with Dex in the back. And for the entire journey, Bennett stared out of the window. The bus was extremely noisy though, with jubilant teammates and cheerleaders.

Kirby didn't know if Bennett knew who he was sitting next to. Every time he glanced back at him, Bennett looked mesmerized.

Within moments, the motion of the bus had lulled its riders into a deep slumber. The five hour journey seemed like five minutes.

"We're here!" Coach yelled.

Generally, when the game was out of town, or if there was a tournament, the team would spend the night at a hotel. Two players were assigned to each room; usually, the guy you rode with was your roommate. This time was no exception. They stayed at a nice one. Each room had double beds that gave electric massages. Just put a quarter into the slot and the bed would vibrate for an hour.

"Yeah, Joe! Here's the station I was lookin' for. Just look at that woman. She's a fox! What a body! Just look!"

"Sh-Sh-She's fine, I'll g-g-give her th-th-that."

"Check out that midget!"

"I se-se-see him."

Interrupted by a knock on the door, Kirby called, "Who is it?" and quickly changed the channel.

"It's me, Bennett."

"Oh," Kirby sighed with relief. "I thought you were Coach."

"Did I disturb you?"

"Naw, man, come on in. We were just watchin' the news... right, Joe?"

"W-W-What? Oh, y-y-yeah, th-th-the news." Big Joe, feeling a bit frustrated, offered, "Y-Y-Yo, I'm g-g-gonna get s-s-some ice."

"All right, Joe." Kirby closed the door and heard Bennett mumble. "I'm sorry."

"Ay, man, that's all right." He turned and they hugged. Tears began to flow down Bennett's face.

"I don't know, Kirby, I don't know, anymore. Things just came down on me so hard."

"I know, man, I know." They separated and Bennett sat on the bed.

"Momma said it was like this for Job. He lost all he had too. But, it seems just so hard for me to handle. And, on top of that," Bennett began to wipe away his tears, "Simon is over there offerin' me the world, if I do what he wants. You should hear some of the stuff he was sayin'."

Bennett explained Simon's whole deal to him. Even about the drugs which he wrestled long and hard with before he eventually flushed down the toilet.

Kirby's spirit was galvanized. "Don't worry, me and the guys are behind you a hundred percent. Me, especially. I'll go down with you. Down!"

"I know, Kirb, thanks."

"Thanks, nothin'. I owe you, remember?" Kirby pointed to a vein in his left arm. The two men hugged again and Big Joe and Dex walked in.

"Aw, ain't th-th-that s-s-sweet?"

"Aw, shut up, Joe. You're just mad 'cause Dex ain't huggin' you."

"Very funny," Dex said.

"Yo! What time is it?" Kirby became very excited.

"It's eleven-thirty." Dex glanced at his watch.

"Let's go knock on doors, and run!"

"Man, Kirby, you crazy. We have the biggest game of our lives tomorrow and need all the rest we can get. I'm goin' to bed and get me a massage." Dex left the room laughing.

"Me, too." Bennett followed and caught the door before it could close.

"That g-g-goes f-f-for me, t-t-too," Big Joe said and crashed onto his bed.

"You guys are a bunch of party-poopers! I'm goin' downstairs," Kirby said.

"L-L-Lock the d-d-door on y-y-your way out and d-d-don't m-m-make any noise w-w-when y-y-you c-c-come back."

"A-A-Aw sh-shut up, ya babblin' idiot," Kirby slammed the door.

While in the hall, Kirby heard some distant music. When he got on the elevator, there was a man wearing a T-shirt and real tight dungarees. Kirby asked him just before pressing the button for the lobby, "Do you know where all the music is comin' from?"

"Sure. It's up on the next floor. My friend is throwing a party in his suite."

"Is it a private party?"

"Yeah...sorta," he said. "But, you're invited."

"Bet! Let's go!"

To where, Kirby didn't know, but when they got there, the guy had vanished. Kirby walked through the dancing crowd.

He couldn't help but notice something strange. He could deal with the fact that there were only two blacks—he and this other dude standing on the terrace. However, he became very uncomfortable when he realized there were no women, especially on the dance floor.

He thought to himself, maybe they were in another room gossiping. That's what he had hoped, anyway. He spotted a bar and headed for it. There were about five or six stools with velvet seats that were unoccupied. He sat in the middle. The bartender approached and asked in a dulcet voice, "What will you have?"

Kirby looked at him strangely, "A Coke please, I'll have a Coke." He thought to himself, Somethin's just not right.

Just as his Coke arrived so did this man-mountain, wearing a pink tank-top shirt and white pants. "Shorty, care to dance?" Kirby almost swallowed his tongue trying to say "no."

"Maybe some other dance, okay Shorty?"

"I don't think so, Horse." Kirby turned back to the bartender who was in a white shirt and black bow-tie. He started sipping his Coke when to the right of him this little pip-squeak, wearing a black leather jumpsuit, sat down.

"Hi, there," he said. Kirby didn't answer, he nodded his head and continued sipping.

Several minutes later, he realized he was on his second Coke. He hadn't paid for it.

"What's goin' on?" Kirby asked aloud to himself.

Kirby and the little guy were still sitting side by side. They were both facing the bar and grooving to the music. Kirby felt something touch him. He turned to his left. Nothing. He then turned to his right and saw it was the pip-squeak's hand. Kirby jumped up and doused him in the face with his Coke.

"Yo, man! I don't play that. What's wrong with you?"

"Nothin's wrong with me. I'm straight!...Full, man!"

Kirby looked around to see if anyone was coming toward him. No one. He spotted the door through the crowd and shot for it like a bullet. He flew down the hallway. The elevator was there. "Thank goodness!" he exclaimed and pressed the lobby button. He had forgotten what floor he was staying on and was huffing and puffing for all he was worth.

He reached the lobby in a matter of seconds. He got out of the elevator, figuring to go outside for a breath of fresh air. There sat Simon and Willie reading magazines.

The clerk was the only other person in the lobby which was carpeted with a shaggy green rug. Kirby quickly pulled himself together and angrily went toward them, "What are you and 'Bubba' doin' here? We don't want you here."

"We who?" Simon said to Willie.

"We!...Me and Bennett...Why don't you crawl back under the rock you came from. Or better yet, go somewhere, and die."

"Look, I'm here to see a ball game...And, secondly," Simon opened his jacket exposing a huge jagged-edged knife, "I don't care who doesn't want me here. I'm here. It's a free country. Didn't they teach you that in school, chump?"

"I'll call the cops, you murderer."

"Please, boy," Simon waved Kirby off.

"Don't you know, you're killin' your own people? First, Stinky, now you're tryin' to destroy Bennett. And who knows how many others you got hooked."

"Who me?"

"Yeah, you! You filth!"

"Ay, I'm just as innocent as a lamb. And just as gentle as a dove."

"You're just as nutty as a fruitcake. And you don't scare me with that knife. I'll still take you apart, or die tryin'."

"Look, boy," Willie added, "I think you better leave while you can."

"You ain't sellin' me no wolf-tickets, 'cause I ain't, buyin' none."

Kirby stood in front of Simon with his fist balled. Willie stared at Kirby making sure he did no damage. "You haven't seen the last of me," Kirby said grudgingly, and walked off.

"So be it." Simon resumed reading.

CHAPTER FOURTEEN

"All right, men," Coach Dee started his homily. "You all know by now Slippery Rock is going to play physical. So we'll have to use speed and defense, and do all the little things—like dive for loose balls and take charges."

The locker room resembled the midget-sized room at Mt. Vernon, but the air was a lot fresher, Kirby thought.

"H-H-How b-b-big is their f-f-f...f-f-f..."

"Front line, Coach?" Kirby interrupted.

"Good question, Joe," Coach Dee said, giving Kirby a hard look. "They go 6-7, 220; 6-11, 250; and 7-1, 270."

"Good God Almighty!" Hezekiah shouted. Sighs of dismay came from the rest of the team, including Bennett, who was usually the coolest when it came to size disadvantage.

"Yes, but they are also very, very slow." Coach smiled. "So here's how we can beat them." He proceeded to draw diagrams of plays on the green chalkboard. For the last time of the season, they huddled together and yelled, "Knights!" The team was so hyped they couldn't wait to get started.

"Bennett, come on! Go left! Go right! Come on, Bennett, pass the ball when you get hung up in the air!" Coach yelled onto the court.

Kirby wasn't himself and his mind clearly wasn't on the game. Not because of Simon. It was a little beyond that. Coach never before had to yell instructions to Bennett. Kirby knew Bennett wasn't throwing the game. It was something about the way those guys were playing him. They weren't playing dirty. But, they just seemed to know every single move he tried and every shot he attempted. It was as if every player had perspicacious instincts.

Bennett received a lob pass from Honey Jack in the post. He faked left and went right and was immediately swarmed. Bennett dribbled the ball down the right baseline, pump faked, and was stripped. Out of desperation he was called for a reach-in foul.

With five minutes left to go in the first half, Bennett was benched after picking up his third foul. Five fouls and you're disqualified. Before the benching, he scored ten points. The team needed every one of them.

"I don't understand it, Kirb. They know my every single move. Nobody has played me that good, ever. I don't understand it."

With Bennett on the bench, Slippery Rock ran off twelve unanswered points. And before Mt. Vernon knew it, they were down by fourteen, 49-35.

"This place reminds me of Westchester County Coliseum," Bennett said as he continued to rub the sweat from his brow.

"Yeah, it does, doesn't it?"

"Ay," Bennett said, "that guy over there..."

"Who? Their coach?"

"Yeah, but not that one. The other one." The coach Kirby was talking about was the head coach. He was a tall man with white hair wearing a beige three-piece suit. The other coach standing next to him was wearing a gray suit.

"The one in the gray."

"Yeah, what about him?"

"He looks familiar," Bennett said thoughtfully, and sat back in the brown vinyl chair. "He looks real familiar."

"It'll come to you after a while."

"I guess."

Three minutes elapsed, and the score remained the same. Both teams were playing very poorly. Suddenly, like a rocket, Bennett jumped from his chair. "I know who he is!"

"Who?" Kirby had forgotten, his mind still wandering.

"He's the guy I played against at Fourth Street that day."

"Bennett! Bennett!" Kirby shouted. But, by the time he shouted "Bennett" for the last time, Bennett was already being held back by Coach Dee, a ref and one of the players. The crowd was enjoying the incident more than the game, especially, since Bennett wasn't playing.

"What's going on?" Coach Dee asked. The melee moved toward the center of the court. Hearing Coach Dee's question, Kirby went over.

"Coach, that guy tricked Bennett into a game of one-on-one so he could study his moves."

"He what!" Coach Dee said.

Tempers finally eased after several minutes of trying to keep Bennett and their assistant coach off one another. The first half ended with the score 55-40. The seven of them—Coach Dee, the two Slippery Rock coaches, the two refs, Bennett and Kirby—met in the long, narrow hallway.

"Who can tell me exactly what happened to cause such an outburst?" the head referee managed to say through his bushy mustache and beard.

"I can tell you exactly what happened!" Bennett said, rudely interrupting the assistant coach who kept shouting that he was attacked by Bennett.

"Don't blame me!" Bennett said and moved in on him. Coach Dee held him back. The assistant coach continued, "I was attacked, by this man...boy rather, because our defense had him beaten down and knew his every move. He took it out on me because I'm the defensive coordinator."

"How did you know his every move so early in the game? We never played before today. Matter-of-fact, how would he know you are the defensive coordinator," Coach Dee added.

When Bennett said, "I'll tell you how he knew," Kirby could see beads of sweat forming on the assistant coach's head. Bennett then related everything about the incident at Fourth Street playground that day.

"Is that true?" the head referee asked the Slippery Rock assistant coach.

"Yes, that's correct."

The second half was delayed about thirty minutes. The crowd grew restless, but they all stayed nonetheless.

Everyone associated in the uproar listened intently. This was an imbroglio, but a decision had to be made. The Slippery Rock assistant coach was ejected from the game for violating ethics code rule number twenty-one. Slippery Rock's head coach was furious. He informed the assistant coach that his services would no longer be needed after the season ended.

It apparently wasn't the first time this had happened. The head referee turned to Coach Dee, "Would you like to protest the game and win by forfeit?"

But before Coach Dee could utter an answer, Bennett shouted, "No! No! No! Coach, let's win this our way."

Coach agreed.

The assistant coach lost control. "You lyin' punk. I had dreams of becomin' a head coach! You messed me up!"

"No! You messed yourself up!" Bennett retorted.

Kirby couldn't help but wonder what Bennett's motives were. Was it the deal with Simon or the school winning its first championship? Kirby analyzed Simon's proposition and how very tempting the offer seemed. It could certainly end most of Bennett's problems.

The game resumed with Bennett sitting on the bench. Coach was making sure he cooled off before he turned him loose. Mt.

Vernon was down 68-50 when Coach finally let him in, with four-teen minutes remaining.

Bennett ran the pick and roll play with Big Joe and picked up a quick two points. Then he came off a screen set by Honey Jack, lost his man and caught Dex's alley-oop pass for a slam dunk. The Mt. Vernon fans were finally back in the game.

Bennett was ubiquitous, and his shots went through the hoop in rapid succession. Within minutes he scored fourteen points. Slippery Rock no longer had their defensive coordinator and their intensity began to wane.

With five minutes left, the score was 84-82, Slippery Rock. At the foul line, Bennett collected his 35th and 36th point. He was perspiring so much, you could see his skin through the white parts of his blue and white uniform.

Kirby kept wondering if Bennett would score more than forty points and help Mt. Vernon win by more than five points. The way he was playing in the second half, he could've scored a hundred points and they could've won by fifty.

Four minutes and fifty seconds went by. All of Kirby's speculating would shortly come to an end. Mt. Vernon took the lead 94-90. With thirty-eight points and just fouled, Bennett had the chance to score two more from the line. The game was almost over, thanks to Bennett and Big Joe's miraculous efforts. Big Joe had eighteen rebounds—six off the offensive board—four blocked shots, twelve points and a school record of thirteen steals.

Bennett went confidently to the line with three-to-make-two. He bounced the ball for an eternity before releasing it. He then stepped away and glanced over his shoulder. Simon was sitting some ten rows behind Mt. Vernon's bench. Kirby gave him a grimace that would've scared off a wild tiger, but it didn't seem to rattle Simon. He just tipped his funny-looking hat toward Bennett.

Back at the line, Bennett bounced the ball for another millennium. This time, the ball twirled around the inside rim and popped out.

He stepped away again and took another look into the bleachers. Simon repeated his ritual, but this time left his seat. Bennett had thirty-nine points and the team was leading by five.

When he stepped back to the line, the bearded ref handed him the ball. Kirby didn't know what Bennett was thinking. Bennett shook his head in bewilderment. "What is he going to do?" Kirby whispered. He waited, sweating in anticipation.

Bennett drummed the ball onto the gym floor. The timing between each bounce shortened and became stronger with the frenzy of the crowd. The crowd roared, "BEN-nett! BEN-nett! BEN-nett!" Coach Dee sat calmly. Coach thought Bennett was trying to make Slippery Rock pay. Kirby knew the real reason.

Finally, the ball was launched, everything else went black. The ball soared through the air for what seemed like forever. But when it found its target, it hit nothing but net. Instantly, the crowd's chants erupted into cheers. The team swarmed all over Bennett; they pushed, hugged and pulled him from all directions. Things couldn't have been better, Mt. Vernon won.

Bennett was selected the Most Valuable Player of the game and was named the National High School Player of the Year. Coach knew about the Player of the Year award, but decided to wait until after the game to tell him. He figured if they'd lost, he could've used the news to cheer him up.

"I knew you couldn't do it," Kirby told Bennett. They embraced in celebration. "I knew you couldn't do it."

"I couldn't risk it, Kirb. I just couldn't risk it. Momma's been too good to me. Dannon and Yvette need me. And you, man," Bennett said, "I didn't want you to lose respect for me."

"Bennett, you know I wouldn't have." They exchanged fives.

On the way to the locker room, Simon stepped out of nowhere with Willie behind him. They stopped Bennett dead in his tracks. "Hey, Youngblood!" Bennett felt a chill run through his body. "Youngblood!" Simon repeated, "you really disappointed me. Nobody does that to me and gets away with it. I let you do it twice.

Now, Blood," Bennett stood firm, looking Simon directly in the eye, "I lost a lot of money. Somebody's gonna pay me."

Bennett watched Simon back slowly into the crowd.

"Simon's a little upset," Bennett said with an unconvincing smile, "claims he wants to get paid."

"Don't worry about that chump," Kirby said just as unconvincingly.

"You think I'm worried?" Bennett said entering the locker room. But this time with more conviction.

Kirby reassured him, "Not at all."

"Ay, Bennett!" Dexter yelled. "Hold up your trophy! A photographer is here!"

"We're number one! We're number one! We're number one!" the team shouted and shouted. The room was vibrating with excitement. The whole team was dancing, throwing towels, slapping fives. A couple of the guys were singing a medley of Jackson Five songs.

"Men, guys, champs. Let me have your attention!" Coach stood on a table in the middle of the locker room. "It's four o'clock now. We have five hours till we leave. Let's all go have Chinese food. On me!"

"Coach Dee! Coach Dee! Coach Dee!" the team chanted.

"That was some good food." Kirby said later back on the bus.

"Yeah, it was," said Bennett.

"Ay man, what's wrong? Did Simon upset you?"

"No."

"Why you so down?"

Bennett blurted out, "Man, it's Tara. I can't feel the full effects of this championship and stuff because she's not here. Kirb, I love that girl...especially what she tried to do about the Honor Society and all. I feel good, but at the same time, I feel like somethin's missin'."

"Yeah, Ben, I know what you mean," Kirby said. The bus was filled with festive noise and celebration. "What do you figure to do about…"

"Say, Kirb, what time do you think we'll get back to Mt. Vernon?"

"Well, it's a five-hour drive and it's nine now. So…"

"Yeah, well, I'm goin' to her house when we get back."

"Tonight?"

"Yeah, tonight. I won't be able to get any sleep if I don't see her."

"I know love makes you do some crazy things, but that's insane…Say Ben, I didn't tell you what happened to me last Saturday. The day it rained cats and dogs."

"What happened, now?"

"Well, check this out…Kathy's parents were supposed to be out of town for the day, and it was our first anniversary bein' together. So we decided that there was no better time to get to *really* know one another for the first time." Kirby gave Bennett a nudge. "You know what I mean?"

"Yeah, man, I know what you mean," Bennett returned the gesture.

"So we got Smokey Robinson and the Miracles playin' and they are kickin' it real smooth. The mood was real nice, you know. We're huggin' and kissin' and what-not, feelin' real good about each other. And, just as I'm about to cross 'home plate,' you know, score that winnin' run, to win the big game, I goes for my wallet. I look and…Bam! I discovered I didn't have my jammie with me! But, I didn't panic, I figured I'd let Smokey bail me out. I contin- ued to absorb myself in the moment. I'm sayin' to myself, yeah Smokey—sing. I look deep into her eyes, givin' her this real sensu- ous look. Like, one of those…'I love you so much, I can't wait for you to be mine' looks. Now, I'm thinkin', thank you, Smokey. Then, Kathy looks deeply into my eyes. She stares awhile; I stare back; she stares again. I'm just starin' away—you know, real sen- sual…allurin'. Then, out of the blue, she nabs me with one of those 'if you think I'm gonna take any chances, you're crazy' looks."

Bennett started cracking up.

"I'm thinkin'...thanks for nothin' Smoke. I wasn't about to take no bus way across town home to get one, so I figured I'd brave the rain, like a man, and haul it to the nearest drugstore...nine blocks away. I'm doin' my famous Jim Brown routine. You know, when he's doin' his thing comin' out of the backfield. I finally make it there...and wouldn't you know it...the store is jam packed! Everybody and their grandmomma was in there. I wasn't about to buy no jammie with all those people in there."

"What'd you do?" Bennett asked, still laughing away.

"I goes over to the paper rack. Man, I must've read every magazine ever known to mankind. Then finally, the store clears out. I picked up a box and goes over to the cash register, to pay for it...Why'd, I do that?...This old bald guy wants to talk. 'You know,' he said, 'you're doin; a good thing. I like to see young men take responsibility. You know, these things here help prevent unwanted pregnancy and stave off diseases. I always tell my, two sons...if you just gotta go deep sea fishin'...wear a protective suit.'

"Bennett, this man went on and on and on. Then, I had to say to him—'cause he wasn't gonna stop—'Mister, with all due respect...I got somewhere to go!' I'm off bravin' that miserable weather."

"Just like Jim Brown?"

"Bennett, you would've been proud. So I was three blocks away...my heart starts to beat fast, in anticipation of the pleasure I'm about to encounter. I'm two blocks away and I'm sayin' to myself, I'm gonna be a happy, young man. Then, I'm about a block away...and Bennett...my heart just stops!"

"What happened!"

"Kathy's whole family! The mother, father, sister, brother and even the dog is goin' inside the house. I said to myself, Ain't this a blip! And that was the end of my romantic celebration that night."

"Only you, Kirb, only you."

"What?" Kirby asked, "Think that could never happen to you?"

Bennett smiled and patted his front pocket.

"You keep yours in your pocket?"

"Ay, you can't always trust those wallets, can you?" The two slapped fives and shared a brief chuckle. Then they realized that they'd exhausted themselves enough for one day, so they decided to get some much needed sleep.

⁂

"Okay, people, let's move it. I got somewhere to go. We have from now 'til Monday to celebrate!" Bennett shouted.

"Somewhere to go this time of mornin'?" Becky said from her seat.

"Yeah," Bennett answered, "but, you wouldn't understand."

"Oh yes, I would, if you told me."

"Maybe next time."

"Yo, Bennett, I'll see you later," Kirby said as Bennett took off down the dark street.

Kirby was summoned to carry Bennett's bags home. Bennett took his two trophies himself. One was for Tara, the other was for protection. The streets were dark and scary.

⁂

"Who in the world is that this time of night?" Mrs. Copeland asked herself walking slowly down the stairs in her robe. "Who is it?"

"Mrs. Copeland?"

Mrs. Copeland, thinking to herself that the voice calling out sounded familiar, inquired, "Yes?"

"It's me, Bennett."

"Tara's Bennett?"

"Yes, ma'am." The door was opened to him. He kissed her on the cheek. "Mrs. Copeland, I'm real sorry, and I'll explain this all later," Bennett said while running up the stairs.

"Wake up, Tara, wake up." Bennett shook her gently.

"Bennett," she said, languid-eyed. "What are you doing on my bed? Where's my mother and father?"

"Your mother's downstairs, and your father's in bed, I guess."

"And what are you doing here this time of night?" Tara turned towards her dresser; the clock set amid perfumes and a picture of Bennett. "Time of morning I mean."

"Tara, see...we won."

"Yeah, I heard about it on the radio, that's nice," Tara mumbled.

"Aren't you happy for me? I was the Most Valuable Player. I was also awarded the National High School Player of the Year."

"Yeah, I'm happy for you. Congratulations," Tara mumbled and turned her back to Bennett.

"I don't blame you for bein' angry with me. Kirby told me what you tried to do for me. I'm happy. I mean...grateful."

"Oh, yeah," Tara mumbled again, her eyes fixed on the pink-draped windows.

"Tara, look, at me."

"What for? I already know what you look like. Boy, do I." Bennett gently turned her face toward his. Tears came to her eyes, "You hurt me, Bennett. The way you were dancing with that Jezebel and her kissing you right in my face."

"I know, and I'm sorry. I'm real sorry. Tara, I didn't feel the full effect of winnin' the championship or the awards because you weren't there to share them with me. I need you Tara, I need you, bad."

"I love you, Bennett. I always did." Tara could no longer control herself. The two embraced one another tightly. She sobbed loudly, "Oh, Bennett, I love you so much."

"I love you, too." Bennett wiped away her tears. "Here, I want you to have this. You're my MVP, baby."

"Bennett, that's yours."

"I know. I want you to have it."

"But, what about, Dannon...what about him? You always..."

"I'll give him the other one."

"You're giving away both trophies?"

"Yes, to the people that gave me somethin'."

"How about Momma and Yvette?"

"That's, another surprise."

"What is it?"

"Well...Coach told me on the way back that after the motorcade, when we get to City Hall, I'll be receivin'," Bennett hesitated, "are you ready for this?"

"Yes, yes, tell me."

"The key to the city!"

"Oh Bennett, that's wonderful! That's wonderful!" Tara again hugged him ardently, nearly choking him to death. "Oh Bennett, that's just great!"

"I better leave now. Your mother's still downstairs. I've been here long enough." Bennett stood up.

"You're not going anywhere until you give me my kiss."

"Tara," Bennett smiled, "you still drive a hard bargain."

"I love you, Bennett."

"I love you, too, and we'll spend the whole day together tomorrow. Just you and me," Bennett said, backing slowly out of the room.

"Bennett, I won't mind if we just stay at your house with your family."

"You sure?"

"Yes, I'm sure," Tara said. "Besides, it's been a long time since I've seen your mother."

"Okay. Good night, sweet princess."

CHAPTER FIFTEEN

Bennett was steadily putting the pieces to his life back together. He and Tara reconciled. He accepted a four-year scholarship from Iona College in New Rochelle, New York. He also got his old job back with more reasonable hours. And, his mother was finally able to receive public assistance to get them out of the rent bind.

He and Tara started talking about marriage again. They were back to their hugging and kissing routine, and the whole school was buzzing about them. They were voted Couple of the Year, beating out pretty Traci TaShawn-Baxter and Alexander Jordan, the homecoming queen and the captain of the football team.

In June, the night before Bennett was to receive the key to the city, Kirby and Kathy decided to treat Bennett and Tara—with the money that Kirby had started saving to buy a car—to dinner at Cromwell's.

"Ay, Tara, remember our big date here?"

"Yeah, we were at the table right over there."

"Remember what happened, Bennett?" Tara asked with a sly smile. Kathy smiled too, but didn't know why.

"What happened?" she asked. Kirby had already heard about it.

"Nothin' much. We just ordered a twenty-two dollar meal, and I found out I'd left my wallet at home."

"Who paid the bill?"

"I did," Tara laughed. "My mother always told me, to have something with me, whenever I went out, just in case."

"Oh, yeah?" Kirby replied. "Then you can pay for these steak dinners. I think I forgot my wallet."

"Forget it," Tara said.

Kirby noticed the puzzled look on Bennett's face. "Hey man, what's up?"

"I don't know, but I feel someone's watchin' me."

"Nonsense...It's just your imagination...I know what it is. You're just worried that Kathy and I might sandbag you guys with the bill."

"Get outta here, you nut," Bennett said.

"Okay," Kirby said. "Maybe, you're just a little nervous about gettin' that key tomorrow."

"Oh, shut up, Kirby," Kathy said. "You talk too much."

"Are you okay, honey?" Tara asked.

"Yeah, baby, I'm okay."

"Ay, what time is it?" Kirby asked.

"It's nine," Bennett said, "and I better get outta here."

"For what?" Kirby said.

"I have a one o'clock appointment with the city tomorrow."

"Nonsense," Kirby said in attempt to lighten his anxiety. "Let's stay just a little while longer."

"Kirby, you're just like a woodpecker...peck, peck, peck."

"Thank you, but we're still stayin'."

They stayed another two hours before Bennett ordered, "Let's go!"

Moments later, the four were strolling along the dark and peaceful streets of downtown Mt. Vernon.

"It feels good out here," Kathy said.

"Yeah, it does feel good," Tara responded.

Arm-in-arm they walked. They were on top of the world, fearing nothing, worrying about no one and just having a good time.

"I got it!" Bennett exclaimed and stopped dead in the middle of the street.

"Got what, honey?" Tara said.

"Let's get outta the street first," Kathy said.

"Blood, whatcha got?"

"Kirb, don't you ever call me that."

"Sorry."

"Anyway, now I know who got Mr. Whitby and Angela in trouble."

"Who?" they said simultaneously.

"It was Miss Peacock!"

"Get outta here. How'd you come to that assumption?" Kirby said.

"I remember, after I left Whitby's room, the hall was empty. But, now I remember walking past Miss Peacock. She must've heard what I was sayin' when I was talkin' out loud to myself. We all know she and Whitby didn't get along too tough."

"Bennett, my boy, you should go on Dragnet."

"Very funny," Bennett said and they continued walking. "Kirby, Kathy, thanks for dinner, and we'll see you tomorrow. And, Kirby, I'm still not lettin' you off the hook for my burgers!"

"Well, baby, tomorrow's your big day."

"Wrong."

"What do you mean?"

Tara and Bennett stood in the doorway, hugging and smooching.

"It's *our* big day."

Tara blushed. "What's wrong, Bennett?"

"I still feel like someone is watchin' me. Man, I feel so uncomfortable, for some reason."

"Do you want to come inside?"

"Naw, I'll be okay. Maybe, Kirby's right, that I'm just a little nervous about tomorrow," Bennett reassured and kissed her good night.

"Good night, celebrity."

CHAPTER SIXTEEN

"Come on, Momma. If you don't hurry up, we'll miss the motorcade. And I'm the guest of honor." Bennett stood at the door with Dannon and Yvette. He was wearing his new navy blue suit.

"Oh, son." Mrs. Wilson left her room closing her pocketbook. "Bennett, you know it's not every day a mother has a son that gets a key to the city."

"Yes, Momma, I know that." Bennett kissed her on the cheek.

"Momma, I gotta go to the bathroom," Dannon said.

"Go when you get back!" Bennett said.

"Go now, Dannon," Mrs. Wilson said smiling.

"Momma, we're gonna miss it!"

"Oh, Bennett, it ain't even noon yet. Motorcade don't start 'til one or one-thirty. Relax, son, you're too nervous."

"See, Bennett, I'm finished."

"Now, I gotta go," Bennett hurried off to the bathroom.

The motorcade was filled with excitement as the team and thousands of Mt. Vernon's faithful well-wishers celebrated. Exuberant people cheered and threw confetti. It started at Kingsbridge Road on the south side and ended on the north side at City Hall. It was a picture perfect summertime day.

The team and Bennett's family (which included Tara) sat on the platform just above the stage. One could see Bennett was extremely nervous, judging by the way he fumbled with his blue and yellow polka dot tie.

"And now," Mayor Sherese Gibson, an extraordinary and distinguished black woman, concluded, "I present to you the man of the hour, Mr. Bennett Mayco Wilson!" The crowd went berserk as Bennett made his way to the microphone. He stood there, motionless, listening to the applause and cheers. His mother was deeply moved. She sat between Coach Dee and Tara.

"Speech! Speech! Speech!" the enormous crowd chanted.

When the applause and cheers subsided, Bennett began to talk. "Good afternoon, ladies and gentlemen." The cheers and applause started all over again.

"Good afternoon, and thank you. Thank you all, for everything...your enthusiasm, your cheers, your support and your pride in our team. Me and my teammates really appreciate this and we are honored. It's a feeling that words just cannot express.

"Um...I...really don't feel worthy of such a prestigious award."

"You're worthy brother man! You are worthy!" a voice cried out from the mass of people.

"Thank you, and...I do accept it, because, I do know, from what my momma taught me, that prayer and a little faith and a lot of hard work, can take you a long way; so maybe, I will feel worthy one day. At least, I hope so.

"Well...wow, I'm not really much for public speakin', but, I do wish to share somethin' with you. Over the past few days, weeks, and months I've learned a lot. A lot about loyalty and respect. About, doin' what's right for your fellow man, and most of all, havin' your own mind.

"I've had it sort of rough these past two months. There were days when I just didn't know which way to turn, left, right, front or back. I just didn't know. There was a night when I actually slept in the gutter. No, not because my Momma put me out or I was homeless. But, because I was so overcome with personal grief and disappointment that," Bennett was overcome with emotion and it looked like everyone in the crowd was ready to shed tears as well, "I just didn't know what to do. But, I looked up! And one thing I'm thankful for, I never, ever, resorted to using drugs or alcohol or any kind of junk like that.

"A lot of you heard of him, but we knew him. He was our teammate, and he was a good friend of mine. Stinky was a talented basketball player. He could do some things on the court that I could only dream about doin'. He was also extremely intelligent. In fact, he was an A student. He just wasn't smart enough to not get hooked on drugs. But, throughout my problems, and unlike my dear friend Stinky...Leonard, I should say...I fought back. And, I hung around the right kind of people. Friends. They are my friends, for sticking by me. A true friend is a person who will stand by you, no matter how heavy the burden is, and do right by you.

"You know, a lot of times," Bennett took time to manage a smile, "I guess some of you older folks will understand this better. But, when you are in a state of confusion and are contemplatin' doin' somethin' wrong—wrong and dangerous—you really need the right kind of person by you. I don't know how I would've made it without you buddy, but, thanks, Kirb. Thanks for bein' there, man.

"And, to all of you teenagers out there, I'm not comin' to you as a person of forty, thirty, or twenty; I'm eighteen years old. My advice to you is don't resort to drugs. Don't get mixed up with anybody or anything that can cost you your future. Your life. If you don't have one now, find a friend. A true friend. One that can and will help you along the way. If you can't find one, learn to be a loner. That probably sounds hard to do, but don't mess yourself up. Let's all come together. Let's recognize that we are the future. Let's do what we have to do. Let's hang in there and fight. Be a winner! Dream! Don't let anyone tell you it's okay to do drugs because they do it. It's not! Drugs make you do crazy things, and they kill. Drugs took away a good and very talented friend of mine. Drugs will win you over, if you don't fight against them.

Bennett took time to step away from the microphone as the applause began to drown him out.

"And, another thing," he continued, "I'm not just a basketball player...I am a person! I have dignity! I have pride! I am a person!" Bennett shouted as he threw his fist in the air.

The crowd went wild. The entire team, Mrs. Wilson, Tara, Yvette and Dannon ran over to him. Bennett and Tara held one another as photographers took pictures.

After a while, Mayor Gibson attempted to take control. She went back to the microphone and prepared to present Bennett and his mother with the sterling silver key to the city. The mayor was obviously touched by Bennett's words.

"I will say this. If I had an opportunity to hand-pick a son, you Bennett Wilson, are the paradigm of a perfect son. I would want him to be just like you." The mayor sparked a rousing ovation. "Mr. Wilson, on behalf of our fair city of Mt. Vernon, I declare this day, June 30th 1973, Bennett Wilson day, and I hereby present to you, the key to the city. The best of luck to you in your future endeavors." The two shook hands and Bennett felt like he was brand new.

Suddenly, the sound of a firecracker snapped in the air, and Bennett slumped to the floor. The key dropped from his hand. The place erupted into bedlam.

"Big-Bra!" Dannon screamed. Mayor Gibson passed out. Mrs. Wilson went into shock and Kirby felt like someone cut out his tongue. He tried to scream as he watched in horror, Bennett trembling in a pool of blood, but there was no sound. Instantly, the police swarmed in from all angles.

The race to the hospital was a complete blur. In the waiting room, Tara was gently slapping Kirby into consciousness. Several hours had passed, and Bennett was fighting for his life in the operating room. Mrs. Wilson, heavily sedated and still in shock, quietly entered the waiting room. Kirby ran to her. They hugged and sobbed together.

"He's gonna be fine, Kirby, he'll be okay. He's tough, real tough," Mrs. Wilson was stronger than Kirby. She patted him on the back, "He'll make it." Behind them, a huge cop with big bulging eyes entered.

"Officer, who shot my baby?"

"Well, ma'am, we don't know just yet. But we're workin' on it. That's the reason I'm here; to find out if there was anyone at any time who threatened Bennett."

The officer's statement sent chills through Kirby's body. He couldn't believe it. He remembered Bennett's dream. He also thought about all those people that had something against him: Simon, Mr. Whitby, Angela, Shorty Stokes and the assistant coach at Slippery Rock. Kirby pulled himself together and told the officer everything he knew.

Several weeks elapsed and Bennett was still hanging onto life by a thread. Although the information the authorities had was thorough, there were no arrests. Bennett had been shot just above the heart. Hooked up to a lifepack, every breath he took was an ordeal. The machine breathed oxygen into his nose.

Mrs. Wilson's blood pressure skyrocketed. Her doctors advised her not to see Bennett every day and to seek counseling. Tara's burden became heavier and heavier as each day passed. She visited the hospital only occasionally, but spent a great deal of time with the Wilsons, seeing to it that Yvette and Dannon were getting along all right.

Kirby though, went to the hospital every day and listened to his buddy babble nonsense. Bennett was out of his mind. Kirby tried having conversations with him, but it was no use. He would ramble on about himself and Dannon, Tara, Kirby—everybody.

Then came the day when Bennett regained consciousness. Kirby walked in and placed Bennett's diploma by his bedside. Bennett, seeing his buddy as he focused, said in a dry and weakened voice, "Kirby, you still owe me a couple of burgers."

Kirby smiled cheerfully. "Man, you don't know how glad I am to hear you say that." But when Bennett added, "Let Billy Thomas know that I won't be able to make his camp next month, and tell Yvette that I'm sorry I won't be there for her birthday in October," Kirby began to get nervous.

"But Bennett, the doctors say you're makin' great progress. Don't talk like that."

"I can't fight much longer."

"But..."

"Listen," Bennett said as the pain began to get the better of him, "look after Momma and Tara for me." Kirby's eyes started to water. "And, tell Dannon that I said, it's not always how long you live, but how well. Tell him I said to live every day as if it's his last. He'll know what you mean."

Bennett took time to breathe as he watched tears stream down Kirby's face.

"Don't leave me, man...not now. Hang on...please. We have too much to do together still," Kirby pleaded. "Let me get the doctor."

"No," Bennett said, "it's too late for that."

Bennett took Kirby's hand and held it as tightly as he could, "I love you, Kirb. You're the best friend anybody could ask for."

Kirby couldn't take it anymore. In haste, he capriciously changed the subject. "Man," he said wiping his eyes, "you look good...real good."

They must've talked nonstop for hours before Bennett finally said he was very tired and wanted to go to sleep. He never heard Kirby say good night. Bennett just closed his eyes and smiled. Kirby knew he'd never open his eyes again.

"Rest in peace, my friend, my hero."

CHAPTER SEVENTEEN

Ten years later, sitting with his old high school friend, Kirby thought, *This place was never the same.* Then he said to Dexter, "Bennett's life had to be an example for others. Have you ever seen anyone else like him?"

"No Kirb. I can't say that I have."

"But now that he's gone, with all these drugs and all sorts of corruption out here, who picks up the slack?" Kirby shook his head in bewilderment. "Who can you trust? Clergy? Politicians? Athletes? Parents? Who do you go to, when you need help? When you need someone to console, counsel, and educate you. Man, I have two young boys to worry about. And, you have a five-year-old daughter. Dex, we can't lose this generation."

"I know...I'm scared to death."

"Ay, fellas," Big Joe said as he walked up. He, like Kirby, sported a five o'clock shadow. "What are you guys up to?"

"Congratulations, man, on the good season you had over there," Dex offered.

"Yeah, Big-Joe, Italy must be treating you real well. You're speaking fluently and everything!"

"Aw, Kirb, I can't c-c-c-complain."

"Stop kidding around, man."

Kirby sat back down after the extended handshake, "We were just sitting here for the past few hours, thinking and talking about the good old days."

"Here," Joe offered Kirby a handkerchief.

"No, thanks, I have one."

"Dex?"

"That's okay, I have tissue."

Kirby looked proudly at his two sons and smiled. "I think I'll shoot some hoops."

"You're gonna shoot hoops, dressed like that?"

"Yeah, Dex, dressed like this. Is that a problem with you?"

"Kirby, after all these years, you're still crazy, but you're still my main man. Wish I could join you, but I'm taking the family out to dinner."

"Dex," Joe said, looking in amazement at how much the two boys had grown since he'd last seen them, "Kirby's only dressed like that just in case those boys of his smoke him. He'd have an excuse."

"I know."

"Get outta here."

Kirby slapped five with the two men and proceeded toward his boys. "Ay, Big-man," Kirby said to Junior who was wearing a blue and white striped Mt. Vernon basketball shirt, "Could I have a shot?"

"Yeah, here, Daddy!"

Kirby started bouncing the ball when Bennie, in a brown T-shirt asked, "Why are you playin' in a suit, Daddy?"

This child reminded Kirby of himself. No matter how hard he tried, he couldn't outshoot his brother.

"Well, partner, I haven't had an opportunity to change and felt like a few shots. Is that okay?"

"Yes, Daddy, it's okay."

"Did I ever tell you guys about Bennett Wilson?"

"No, all we hear of is Dannon Wilson, he's the best ballplayer Mt. Vernon ever had," Junior said. Kirby smiled.

"Was Bennett Wilson a basketball player?" Bennie asked.

"Well, he was Dannon's older brother and, he!...was the very best ever!"

"Better than you, Daddy?"

"Better than me? Of course, he was!" Kirby said. "He taught me everything I know." Kirby walked towards half court. "Here's where we stood to shoot and bet burgers on. I always lost because I always missed."

"You gonna try it now Daddy?"

"You think I should?" Kirby said after thinking the question over. And before he could get an answer he offered, "I think I will."

He took off his jacket and gave it to Junior. "Well, Bennett," Kirby said looking at the heavens above, "I never made this shot before, but now, my friend, this one is for you." He settled himself into position and tossed it.

"All right!" they shouted.

Here was serendipity at its best.

EPILOGUE

What we have here, is but a few days...

God has blessed America. After all, millions upon millions flock to this country, legally and illegally, yearning for freedom and searching for the riches which they believe exist here.

We are a leader in just about every technical and scientific area. We are able to give aid to other countries. One of our landmarks exhorts, "Give us your tired, your poor, your huddled masses yearning to breathe free."

All this and we, as a people, tarnish it with drugs and alcohol. When is this going to cease? Each year—too often—someone loses a family member, a close friend or a neighbor due to this "disease of nonsense."

We, in society, especially in our homes, churches and schools have to continue to teach, preach and educate our future and existing America that drugs and alcohol are *dangerous*. They destroy families, ruin individuals and tear up communities. But most of all, they cause death needlessly.

Young America—we have it better than our founding fathers. They pioneered so that we may have this opportunity for a better way of life. With the technology and other resources we have, we can achieve anything. Don't let yourself down. Stay in school and *do the smart thing*—you'll be happier in the long run.

If you need help in recovering from drug or alcohol abuse, please speak with someone: a minister, parent, politician, teacher, older brother or sister, a trusting friend or counselor at any local drug and alcohol clinic. *Get help! It can't hurt!!*

TOPICS OF DISCUSSION

1. The importance of a good relationship between parent and child.
2. The importance of *fair* play. Going through life without having to cheat.
3. Saying "NO" to drugs, by realizing why they're wrong.
4. Saying "NO" to alcohol, by realizing it's not the answer.
5. Saying "NO" to guns, by realizing violence creates more violence.
6. The importance of having the "right" kind of friends.
7. The ability to realize that you are your own person, and not let peer pressure become an endangerment to you.
8. Making every day count toward working at a positive goal.
9. The importance of staying in school.
10. The significance of avoiding unplanned teenage pregnancy.

DISCUSSION QUESTIONS

1. Would you have been as strong in saying "no" to Simon's proposition as Bennett? Why or why not?

2. What kind of decision would he have made by taking the easy way out? Explain.

3. Could you be a dear and true friend to someone the same way Kirby was to Bennett? Why or why not?

4. Why do you think Bennett did not make a mistake and impregnate Tara, although he was madly in love with her?

5. What did Bennett propose to do for his mother when she was hit with severe financial problems? Explain.

6. Would you have proposed to do the same thing? Why or why not?

7. What type of example did Bennett set for his two younger siblings? Explain.

8. If you are an older child, what kind of example are you setting?

9. If you are an only child, what type of example are you setting for other people around you?

10. After Bennett lost everything, how was he able to find strength in what his mother said regarding his problems?

11. Although Bennett was a troubled youngster, what type of outlook on life did he have?

12. Are you making every day count toward achieving a positive, goal? Explain.

13. What effect did Stinky's death have on Bennett?
    What effect did Stinky's actions, including his death, have on the rest of the student body?

14. What point did Bennett direct toward his generation during his speech just before receiving his prestigious key to the city?

15. What feeling do you think Bennett had when he received the key to the city?

16. What did the old man in the drugstore mean when he said, "I tell my two sons, if you're gonna go deep sea fishing wear a protective suit"?

17. Do you think that Kirby's trip to the drugstore to purchase condoms was commendable or stupid because of the end result? Explain.

ACKNOWLEDGMENTS

One thing I realize—racism is alive and well, but when you have black and white or any other mix of nationalities, colors, religions or creeds working together, striving toward making something positive, beautiful things will happen.

The following people, I wish to thank:

Bishop W. McCollough–the deceased leader of the United House of Prayer for All People. A great man who showed me the pathway to Jesus Christ. I especially want to pay homage to him for having seen this confused, frightened, and unstable teenager who was living away from home, attending Norfolk St. University in Virginia and for looking him in his eyes, slapping him on his shoulder and telling him in a profound way that he wanted to make a man out of him.

Bishop S.C. Madison–the succeeding leader of the United House of Prayer. Showing what the words *love* and *courage* are all about.

Pamela Hoover–my wife, who has put up with me all this time. For sticking with me through thick and thin.

Hilda Hoover–my mother, who successfully, single-handedly, struggled to raise two children: Traci and myself—sometimes eating the hole and giving us the donut.

Traci and Sherese Hoover–two of the finest little sisters in the world.

The Blount and Harris and Hoover clans–my family.

The Bronx Band–my brothers in Christ.

All of my brothers and sisters of the United House of Prayer for All People.

All of the people who served as my typist at some time or another during my thirteen year quest to become a published author: Pamela Hoover, Hilda Hoover, Margaret Oliver-King, Lillian Spinelli, Doreen Cano-Colon.

All of the people who served as editors and advisors to me: Ronald Stephenson—my older cousin, who at some point was a father figure, big brother and counselor to me. Thanks for taking that little seventeen-year-old boy seriously when he called you up that night in October of '83 and told you he wanted to write a book. For reading that first draft and sensing that I hadn't read a book in a while, and becoming so disgusted that you kept it from me and made me read five books before you returned it. What a difference reading made. Also thanks to Evelyn Phipps, Martha Corpus, and Jack Howley. To the Editorial Dept—Rennie Browne and David King, the people who taught me the nuances of writing. Claire Harris, the lovely woman who gave me writing tips from a female and African American perspective.

When you strive to accomplish something positive, you need all the encouragement you can get, so I want to thank: Charles Weathers, an upright and very positive brother; James and Laura DeMilio-Trotta, my tenth grade English teacher and his madam; and Paul Wray, my former supervisor and a real genuine person for being there and helping in any capacity. Mrs. Alice Jordan, my twelfth grade English teacher, and the one who encouraged me to join the MVHS Literary Club, thus adding to the exposure of my endeavor. Craig Howell, my cousin, buddy, friend, brother...sparmate. Greg Washington, my childhood buddy, who strived to open doors for me.

I must also give a special thanks to Tony Fiorentino—the 1984 Westchester County Coach of the Year of the Mt. Vernon Knights (currently an assistant coach and scout for the NBA's Miami Heat) for allowing me to be a part of the team, in my attempt to gain insight as to how a high school basketball team functions. His assistant (now Head coach of the 1991 undefeated New York State Champs) Marshall Reiff for giving me tips and explanations during game situations.

Finally, I particularly wish to give thanks to two people—my hero and heroine—whom I love dearly: my grandparents, Percel and Hilda (Chick) Johnson. Thank you, for giving Craig, Traci and myself enjoyable childhoods. Always new outfits on Easter. Always gifts for our birthdays. Always plenty of food on the table for Thanksgiving. Always plenty of presents under the tree. Always being there.

And...Thank You Francis Blount!!!

Your Comments Are Welcomed...

I sincerely hope you've enjoyed reading my novel as much as I enjoyed writing it. And to that end, I invite you to share any comments, questions, or suggestions with me:

Jerald LeVon Hoover
c/o Winston-Derek Publishers Group, Inc.
P.O. Box 90883
Nashville, TN 37203

JERALD LEVON HOOVER was born December 3, 1965 in New York City. He is an award winning writer, named Best New Male Writer of the Year for 1993 by the Literary Society and a recipient of President Bill Clinton's Writer Corps award in 1994. A musician also, Jerald serves as a trombonist in the United House of Prayer for All People. This is his first published novel. He and his wife Pamela, along with their son Jordan, live in upstate, NY.